"Why didn't you tell me who you were?"

Michael didn't answer immediately, and that in itself was a bad sign. Was he judging which answer would work best with her, Pamela wondered bitterly.

"I thought we shared a special moment," he said finally. "It didn't occur to me at the time that you might want references."

"So you trespassed on my land," she said. *And on my heart,* she might have added. Fire simmered behind her dark eyes. "You bought White Acres behind my back. Yet when you saw me again last night, you were ready to take me off with you, knowing I didn't have any idea who you were."

"Why did you come back?" she'd asked him at the time.

"To find you," he'd answered.

And she'd believed him!

Tears of Gold

Helen Conrad

Harlequin Books

TORONTO • NEW YORK • LONDON
AMSTERDAM • PARIS • SYDNEY • HAMBURG
STOCKHOLM • ATHENS • TOKYO • MILAN

ISBN 0-373-02731-1

Harlequin Romance first edition December 1985

CHAPTER ONE

PAMELA STARBUCK looked as though she'd stepped off a page of a high-fashion magazine. Her white dolman-sleeved dress with its persimmon-colored sash had been designed by Riaz, and her wide-brimmed hat was set at an angle over her eye that just barely let her see where she was going. It looked very sexy. Philip had said so, and he wasn't a man for compliments.

But it wasn't "sexy" Pamela was trying to achieve. Dramatic, yes. Nostalgic, certainly, for a time gone by. A fitting tribute to the house, the land, the life that was coming to an end. No one had to know that everything she was wearing had been purchased by her mother years earlier on her honeymoon in Paris. Pamela Starbuck could no more afford finery like this than she could swim the Channel, but she'd wanted to wear something special to host her last party at White Acres, and there the clothes had been, hanging in her mother's closet in the room so unused for so long. Luckily, as the saying went, what comes around goes around, and the same styles popular when her mother was young looked suddenly fresh.

The party was going very well. The guests appeared to be enjoying themselves. The atmosphere was light and fun, and the decorations set a colorful tone. Flowers floated in the pool. Had anyone guessed they'd been strewn strategically to hide the places where the grouting had worn away? It had been a long time since the Starbucks could afford to hire repairmen for luxuries.

An elaborate buffet was set along the side of the pool. Couples strolled about grounds that were not as well manicured as they'd once been, but probably no one noticed. Music was provided by a group of local high-school kids who'd formed a jazz band, not by the professionals who would have been flown in from San Francisco in her mother's day. But it was good music, light and mellow. Just the sort of thing to keep spirits high.

Pamela wandered among her guests, managing to speak to each one in turn without getting bogged down in any extended conversations. At this moment, it was Bernice Walden who'd caught hold of her arm.

"Pamela, darling, the crepes are divine. You must tell me the name of your caterer." Bernice collected facts about other people's households the way a pack rat collected shiny objects. Her pale eyes glittered in anticipation.

Pamela's smile was bittersweet. "It's a family secret, Bernice. Maybe I'll give it to you as a wedding present when you and Fred name the date." With an affectionate tap on her friend's shoulder, she moved on, smiling at one guest after another.

Wouldn't Bernice be surprised to find Pamela's own name tucked inside the envelope? She and her seventeen-year-old sister, Suzy, had stayed up most the night preparing the crepes and all the other food everyone was gobbling down so lustily. She'd hired waiters for the day, but then the money had just about run out.

"Pamela, I really must have a moment alone with you." The man who spoke was in his mid-thirties, but something about his demeanor made him seem older. He was handsome, gray at the temples and dressed very nicely in a tailor-made suit. He looked at Pamela, lines of worry creasing his brow.

She sighed. "I'm sorry, Philip. I really haven't a moment right now. Maybe when the coffee's served?"

Philip Halston unfortunately just wouldn't believe she wasn't going to marry him. He owned the neighboring ranch and had offered to buy out the Starbuck place. There was only one condition. Pamela must come with it.

By the next day it would be too late. The next day, White Acres was going on the open market. The home she'd loved for all her twenty-five years, the land that had been in Starbuck hands since the middle of the nineteenth century, was going to belong to a stranger. This party was definitely her last hurrah.

"Pammie! Disaster! We're out of ice!" Suzy was as blond as a sunny day. Her blue eyes were filled with horror at the thought of iceless drinks, and Pamela almost laughed, but stifled it in time. Seventeen was a touchy age. No sense of humor. It wouldn't do to let Suzy know how funny she was.

"Look in the freezer on the service porch," she told her instead. "I stocked it myself."

"You think of everything." Suzy smiled broadly. "Good thing you have that wart on your nose. Otherwise people might get the idea you were just about perfect."

Pamela grinned, watching her fly off for the service porch, chastising herself for thinking Suzy had no sense of humor. Then she found herself surreptitiously touching her nose with one tentative finger, just in case a wart had sprouted when she wasn't looking.

Perfect. She was hardly that. A perfect woman would have found a way to save the family land. And a perfect hostess would be constantly mingling with her guests. Instead, she was wandering away from them. In a moment, she would be out of sight of the house.

And then she was. Her soft leather shoes were sinking, heel first, into the soil with every step, but still she walked. She had to get away, go up onto the hill that surveyed the valley, have a moment's peace with herself. She couldn't face one more question about the exciting new life she'd soon be launched into.

"Where will you go, Pamela? What will you do?" Everyone wanted to know, and she hadn't a clue.

She climbed the hill slowly, her destination the old fake wishing well that sat at the top. Built of stone, it had been there for longer than she could remember and had never contained a drop of water, except after a rain, when her father would pour in oil to kill the mosquito larvae. But it looked authentic. Too bad it didn't seem to have the power to grant wishes anymore than it had water.

She'd meant to turn and look back at the house when she got to the top. Look back, and maybe cry a little. But the first thing she saw was a man coming through the meadow from the area of the river, and once she saw him she forgot all about her plan.

He was just a stick figure at first, a black line against the white flowers that dotted the green cover of meadow grass. As she watched him come closer, the features of his face began to appear, then the expression. For some reason, his approach fascinated her, held her spellbound. She had no idea who he was, but she wanted to know, and it didn't occur to her to wonder why.

He came straight for her. He might have stayed in the lowland and gone on to the house, but he walked up the hill instead, as though he was irresistibly drawn toward her, forgetting any other goal he might have had.

He was tall—six feet at least, with shoulders as broad as the sky behind him. He was dressed like any river traveler in faded jeans and a chambray work shirt. He certainly wasn't starched looking, but then, men who came from the river seldom were. When he was close enough, she could see that he hadn't shaved for a few days. But she soon forgot these minor drawbacks. Once she'd met his gaze, his eyes were what captivated and held her.

"You're trespassing," she said as soon as he was near enough to hear her.

"Am I?" He kept coming. His eyes were of a blue so brilliant that they seemed to shine from his face. His hair was dark, curly, mussed, a bit too long at the neck, falling in careless disarray over his forehead. His skin was tanned, as though he'd spent a lot of time chasing dreams on the river. But his eyes...They spoke to her before he actually said a thing.

She wondered briefly why she wasn't afraid. There had been violent men who'd come from the river onto her family's land. Once her father had warned one off with a shotgun. But more often they were men out panning for gold, hoping to relive the glory days of the gold rush a century before, or just looking for a little fun. But one never knew these days. And yet, she wasn't for a moment afraid.

"Are you lost?" she asked as he came up in front of her.

"Not anymore." It was a simple statement, made complex by what his eyes were saying. He was a very attractive man, rough appearance notwithstanding. And his eyes said he thought she was was pretty attractive, too.

He stood not three feet away, and she leaned against the stones of the wishing well, gazing at him with as much interest as he showed for her. Silence stretched between them, but there was no awkwardness. She knew that he found it odd to see her there, on the top of a hill, dressed for the city, but that he was rather pleased.

"Making a wish?" he asked at last, gesturing toward the well.

She smiled and for once felt no bitterness. "It's too late for wishes," she said.

He reached to take hold of the rope that held the rotting bucket. "It's never too late for wishes," he said. His blue eyes narrowed. "Tell me yours and I'll make them come true."

She stared at him, then began to laugh. "That's a dangerous promise to make. What if I held you to it?"

He shrugged, his eyes burning. "Try me."

Outrageous. That was exactly what this situation was. There she stood, talking in riddles to a man she'd never seen before. She wondered for a moment if she were dreaming, if this were just some sort of escape her mind had manufactured to release her from the overwhelming loss she faced. But no. There was nothing dreamlike about this man. He was all bone and very substantial flesh. She didn't think she'd ever seen anyone more masculine. He might be the sort of man women dreamed of, but he was all reality.

A gust of wind slapped at her and she reached up to hold her hat to her head, but her gaze never left his. "Try me," he'd challenged. "I don't think I dare," she answered at last.

He shrugged his broad shoulders, opening his palms. His hands were wide but the fingers were long and tapered. An artist's hands. A dreamer's hands. "Nothing ventured, nothing gained," he said.

She smiled and looked away. The wind was ruffling the tops of the trees. She looked out toward the snow-capped mountains, then down toward the flat central valley. "Is there a storm coming?" she asked, shivering slightly though the breeze was warm.

"Yes," he answered softly, but he didn't look toward the gathering clouds, and she knew he was referring to another sort of upheaval. "I think I can feel one coming on."

It was exciting, the way he kept giving everything she said a deeper meaning. She didn't feel threatened by him, but she definitely did feel thrilled. There was a singing in her veins, a bright bubbly feeling that raced and surged and filled her with delicious adrenaline. She didn't think she'd ever felt this way with a man before. She'd never felt this free, this close to a dangerous edge. She'd always kept herself so safe before. She'd never known that taking chances could be this wonderful.

But she was still Pamela Starbuck, the careful one, the responsible one. Thrilled as she was, she couldn't quite let go completely. "What will you do if it hits?" she asked, insistently referring to reality and not the intangible currents he alluded to. She assumed he was camped down by the river, his raft tied nearby. A storm could prove dangerous to him there.

But he wasn't careful at all. He refused to consider the practical. He took her words for a continuation of the conversation he'd begun. His smile, as he answered her, was achingly direct. "When it hits, I'll ride it out the way a surfer rides a wave," he said meaningfully. "How about you?"

Her heart was pounding so loudly that she was sure he heard it. Did he think she was impossibly naive? She knew she was. And yet she didn't feel that he was laughing at her. She felt, in an odd sort of way, that she could trust him with her innocence. She raised her face to the breeze and closed her eyes. "I don't know," she whispered. "I've always been protected before." She wasn't sure just what she was saying, but it seemed to fit the moment.

"I'll protect you." His voice was low, and it seemed to vibrate through her body. "I'll hold you high above the surf, and when the big waves come, we'll take them together."

Insanity. That was what this was. Total insanity, to be talking to a stranger this way. And yet…it felt right. Maybe she needed a little insanity this evening. The last night she would spend on White Acres when she could truly call the place her own. Oh, if only she didn't have to face it!

Maybe she should run away. Maybe she should run away with this compelling man. He was implying all sorts of things with his suggestive talk. She doubted if he really meant much of it. He was having fun with her, just as she was having fun with him. Neither expected the other to take it seriously. But what if she did?

What would he do if she asked to go with him down the river? Her heart began to race at the thought. She could go with him, escape from the guilt and the worries that were tearing her apart. She could leave it all behind and run away, run wild, run off with this river pirate and never look back.

River pirate. She smiled slowly. That's what he made her think of, despite his work clothes. Beneath the denim beat a heart as colorful and flamboyant—and as passionate—as a buccaneer. She was sure of it.

"Is that yours?" He nodded toward the house.

She turned and looked at it, smiling. How she loved the old white elephant! It stood, proud and elegant, as it gleamed in the sunlight, its many columns so neat and orderly.

"Yes," she breathed.

"I thought as much," he said. "It looks as out of place with its surroundings as you do."

She laughed again. How strange. She'd laughed twice now. The man must be magic. She hadn't laughed in days, weeks. Ever since old Mr. Harding, her family's financial adviser, had told her there was no longer any hope, that White Acres must be sold to pay the back taxes. And here she was laughing at everything this river pirate said. Either he was magic, or she was hysterical.

"What would you have put there?" she asked. "What would go with the area?"

He tilted his head to the side, considering. "Adobe," he suggested slowly. "A Spanish courtyard. Maybe even California ranch style. But hardly this."

She shrugged, not in the least offended. He was right, after all. "But this is home to me," she told him. "This looks exactly right."

"It certainly looks like the home of someone who doesn't follow fads," he mused. "Someone with a mind of his own. Or her own." He smiled at her. "Someone who reveres tradition. His own tradition. An individualist."

"That's the way we Starbucks are," she told him, chin high. "We go our own way, and we're proud of it."

His smile crinkled the corners of his eyes. "Let me guess," he said. "The original Starbuck was a Southern gentlemen. Am I right?"

"I can't imagine how you figured that out," she chortled. "Something about the Southern plantation style of architecture?"

He nodded. "Could be." His grin was wide and warm, white teeth flashing against tanned skin. "But I like to think it had more to do with my naturally fine intuition."

He had a sense of humor, too. His smile was attractive. His voice was warm and comforting. But there was nothing comforting about his eyes. They were sharp and knowing, sensual and provocative. She'd never seen a man who intrigued—and on a certain level, frightened—her more.

She leaned against the pillar that held the little roof over the wishing well and closed her eyes for a moment, dreaming. Why not run away with him? She could think of nothing more tempting.

Pamela had never done anything wild in her life. She'd always been the elder daughter, the big sister, the one everyone else relied on. And where had it got her, she whispered to herself silently. Maybe it was time to do something wild and wonderful.

But no. Inside, she was a lot like the dress she was wearing: clean and proper and classically elegant. Ageless, reliable, and just a bit untouchable. Men had often been interested in her, but she couldn't remember any who'd been as familiar from the start as this one had—as though he'd known her before, as though he knew who she was and what she wanted. Even she didn't really know.

He was leaning against the well beside her, arms folded across his chest. His profile was as handsome as the front view, chin strong, nose chiseled, eyebrows dark and silky. "What was it like growing up in a Southern mansion set in the midst of California gold country?" he asked softly. "Was it Spanish moss and mint juleps, or corn tortillas and golden poppies?"

"A little bit of everything." She smiled, remembering. "But the Southern heritage has been diluted, I'm afraid. After all, it's been more than a hundred years."

"Beautiful land," he murmured, shading his eyes and looking out over it. "What's it called?"

"White Acres. Benjamin Starbuck, my ancestor who built the house, named it for the mariposa lilies that bloom every spring, coating the hills."

He nodded. "I can see where you used to ride your ponies." He pointed toward a trail leading across the far hills in the direction of the highway. "Am I right?"

She looked, remembering all those youthful times when she had guided her horse down that dirt path toward playmates, or town, or a swim in the reservoir on a hot dusty day. "Your impeccable intuition wins again."

"And over there—" he pointed across the meadow "—beneath that big old pepper tree. That looks like a perfect place for a lovers' rendezvous."

She smiled as her eyes followed his gesture. "For a picnic?" she suggested.

"That," he agreed, turning to look at her, "and...other things that lovers do."

She felt herself blushing and wished she hadn't. Did he think she'd met lovers there? Well, he could think again. She'd never known a man she'd even consider meeting in such a place. That is, she corrected herself ruefully, she'd never known such a man until now.

Yes, she could readily imagine meeting this one beneath the tree. She could see him waiting there, watching her approach, and her heart beat faster with the image.

"I have a theory about women with eyes as dark as yours," he was saying softly, moving closer all the while.

"Oh?" she said, watching him, not moving away. "What's your theory?"

He was so close she could almost feel him, though he wasn't touching her. Yet his body seemed to be communicating with hers, much the way his eyes were, on some level other than the verbal. She wanted to touch him, reach out and run a finger along the line of his temple, catch his pulse against her palm, mate heartbeat to heartbeat. If only she dared.

Suddenly he reached up and swept her hat from her head, sending her auburn curls cascading down across her shoulders, tumbling in the breeze. She threw her head back and met his gaze, not protesting.

His eyes were dark, the color of blue velvet, and he was leaning even closer, letting his glance caress her neck, the curve of her cheek. Then he spoke again, his voice low and husky.

"I have a theory that on certain nights when the moon is right, those eyes can see deep into a man's soul and read his innermost thoughts—know his secrets better than he knows them himself."

He was so close now that she could feel the heat of his breath against her cheek. She wanted to lift her face to it, close her eyes and turn into his kiss. If only she dared.

"What do you think of my theory?" he prodded.

"I don't know," she answered weakly, avoiding his eyes. All she could think of was the strength of his muscular arms around her. Would he hold her tightly? Would his hands move across her back? Would she curl her arms around his neck and pull him closer still?

"I guess I'll have to test it out on some full-moon night." He held her hat in his hand, but still he hadn't touched her.

"There's going to be a full moon tonight," she said breathlessly.

"Yes." His gaze skimmed over her face, taking in every feature like a man hungering for something. "I know."

She lowered her eyes so that she wouldn't have to see the emotion in his. He would kiss her now if she let him. All she had to do was part her lips, lower her lids, maybe smile. And he would wrap her in his arms and carry her away. Her heart was pounding like a war drum. She wanted him to touch her, hold her, kiss her. But did she dare let him?

He was a total stranger, a man off the river. Was she insane? Yes, that was it. Temporary insanity. Enough to acquit in a court of law, but not enough to soothe her own conscience. She couldn't let this go on. She had to do something to diffuse the intensity. Casting about wildly, she came upon something to say.

"I...I have a theory, too." She swallowed, hoping he didn't notice how shaky her voice was. Gathering courage, she looked directly into his face and barely smiled. "It has to do with men with black hair and eyes as blue as sapphires," she said, her voice becoming stronger. "It concerns Irish ancestry and something called a Blarney stone." She managed a grin and was gratified to see that her statement had the desired effect of putting a little space between the two of them.

"Your intuition isn't bad, either." He seemed to sense what she was doing and didn't force himself on her. He pulled back, looked at her for a long moment, then stuck out his hand. "Michael Donovan's the name."

That changed everything. It was as though they'd been floating on a huge balloon, and someone had put a pin to it. They weren't floating any longer. They were quite solidly back to earth.

"Pamela Starbuck," she replied. Her hand disappeared into his and she watched it go, a little alarmed. "I...I really should get back to my party."

He wasn't releasing her hand. His eyes were searching hers, looking for something in their dark depths. He didn't speak and she began to feel uncomfortable.

"Would you like to come down to the house?" she asked tentatively. "Would you like a drink? Something to eat?"

He shook his head slowly. "No," he said softly. "I've got to get back myself."

Back to what? She glanced at his hand, suddenly afraid to see a wedding ring or some other ill omen, but there was nothing.

"Someone is coming for you." He nodded toward the house, and Pamela turned to see Philip striding across the meadow. "Happy full moon," he said, a wisp of a smile bending his wide mouth. Then he raised her hand to his lips and gently kissed the fingers, handed back her hat and turned to go. In another second, he was off down the hill, whistling as he went.

Pamela watched him, the fingers he'd kissed pressed to her lips. Like a river pirate, he'd come out of the wild to offer her an escape. Now he was going back. Why wasn't she going with him?

CHAPTER TWO

"WHO WAS THAT?" Philip came up behind her, puffing a little from exertion.

"Hmm?" She turned to greet him, her smile distracted. "Oh. Just some river pirate."

"What?" Philip had very little imagination. His cheeks were reddened, and he pulled out a handkerchief to wipe his face. "Tramp, you mean. I'll call the police when we get back to the house."

"No," Pamela said hastily, fingering the wide brim of her hat. "Don't do that. He's perfectly harmless."

She watched as Michael Donovan reached the edge of the clearing. Just before he entered the woods, he turned and stood for a moment, looking back at her. Slowly he raised a hand. Slowly she raised hers in return. Then he vanished into the forest.

"What did you do that for?" Philip was truly bewildered. He peered at the area where Michael had disappeared. "Do you know him?"

"Sort of." She smiled at her friend, feeling a sudden warmth for him. "Come on. I've been away from my guests too long."

"Pamela." His kindly eyes were filled with concern. He put a hand on her arm. His fingers were cool and emotionless, and she remembered how hot and exciting Michael's hand had been. "I know why you're out here. I know how upset you are over losing

White Acres. And you know…you know I'm ready to do my part to keep the land for you. All you have to do—''

She stopped him with a quick hug. "Oh, Philip, you are so dear. You deserve better than a wife like me." He certainly deserved a woman who loved him, a woman who tingled when he touched her. Not one who wanted to stay an arm's length away. They'd known each other forever, but it was only in the past year that Philip had decided they should get married. She wasn't really sure why. When she came right down to it, she doubted if he felt any more passion for her than she did for him. He probably just felt she would make the right kind of wife. Or perhaps he felt sorry for her.

He wanted to protest her statement that he deserved better, but she shook her head. "Let's go down," she said. "I want to join the party."

He trudged along beside her obligingly enough, but he was a bit grumpy. "I liked your hat better on your head," he said, glancing at her sideways.

She laughed and threw her head back, letting her auburn curls toss in the wind. "I'll just bet you did," she agreed. She threw her hat high in the air and caught it as it came sailing back down. Her heart felt light and free.

"Thank you, Michael Donovan," she whispered to herself. "If I ever see you again, I'll have to thank you in person." And she smiled, ready to face her party again.

IT WAS TOO BAD that the carefree mood Michael Donovan had created couldn't last through the next day.

But nothing could soften the pain of signing the papers to put White Acres up for sale.

At least she got a good night's sleep. Her dreams were a swirl that seemed to be part Civil War drama, part New Orleans pirate adventure, all very exciting and unreal. She couldn't remember much about them when she woke, but she could remember the man who'd sparked them.

Michael Donovan. She lay in bed later than usual recalling the way he looked, the sound of his voice, the way he moved. Had he been real? She'd never met any other man who'd stayed in her mind this way. A man who wove himself into the fabric of her thoughts. She could close her eyes and picture him just the way he'd been in the sunshine, tall and strong, black hair, blue eyes, and a smile that sent a tingle through her veins. Had he been real? Or had he just been an illusion, created by her need for solace in a time of distress?

Reluctantly she left thoughts of Michael Donovan behind and got up to face the worst day of her life. It started with a fight she could have avoided if only she'd prepared Suzy better. But she'd assumed that her sister understood just how serious things were. She'd known what the party was all about. Unfortunately she refused to believe it.

"You can't mean it." Suzy's face turned pale when Pamela told her Mr. Harding would be arriving at ten o'clock with the papers. "You're not really going to do this."

"I don't have much choice."

They were sitting at the table in the breakfast room. Morning sunlight streamed in all around them, glinting through the hanging plants that dripped greenery to the floor. Two yellow canaries sang in their cage, perched high among the philodendrons.

"But we've been economizing." Suzy threw her arms wide, her eyes puzzled. "I haven't been out to lunch for ages and I got the summer job at Barbi's Dress Shop."

"I know." Pamela reached across the table and covered her sister's hand with her own. "And I appreciate how hard you're trying."

"And we made all that food for the party ourselves." Suzy's voice was almost a wail of despair.

"Thanks again. But, darling, what we've saved doesn't come anywhere near the thousands of dollars we need to pay the back taxes."

Suzy's eyes were brimming with tears. "That was daddy's fault, not ours. I don't see how they can make us pay."

There was hardly any point in answering that. "They can," Pamela said wryly, "and they will."

"I thought..." Suzy swallowed hard. "I thought you'd do something to stop it."

Pamela wanted to run away and crawl into bed, to hide under the covers and never come out. Instead, she managed a semblance of a smile. "I guess I'm not so perfect, after all," she said softly.

"Almost perfect," Suzy said grudgingly, her face rebellious. "You'd be totally perfect if only you'd marry Philip."

Pamela sighed, looking out over the lawn. "You know I can't do that."

Suzy held back the words for a moment, but the effort was obviously too much for her. "Why not?" she burst out at last. "What are you waiting for? What do you want? How can you do better than Philip?"

Pamela rose and walked to the window. "I thought it was the young who believed in love," she said sadly.

"Oh, love." Suzy tossed the concept away with a toss of her head. "You're too old for that, anyway."

Oh, the lofty perspective on life from the vantage point of seventeen years. Pamela burst out laughing.

"I'm what?" she turned, still chuckling, and Suzy had the grace to look a bit shamefaced.

"You know what I mean. By the time a woman gets to be twenty-five, she has to start thinking about the future, about what's good for her. She can't just go falling in love with any guy who comes along."

Any guy who comes along. For some reason, a perfect picture of Michael Donovan cartwheeled through her mind at those words. She quickly shook her head to dispel the image.

Mr. Harding was on time. He always wore a black suit, summer or winter, and was never so much as a minute late. He had all the papers in his briefcase, and Pamela signed them, one after another.

He'd assured her that there would be no problem in finding a buyer. White Acres lay just off one of the main roads leading into popular Yosemite Valley. It was a prime area.

"Your place will go into multiple listing right away," he told her efficiently. "It will probably be a few days before any agents bring prospective buyers around, but they'll call first to let you know when they're coming. I'll go ahead and put up signs near the road."

Strangers tramping through the house, scuffing the floorboards her great-great-grandmother had oiled with such care, fingering the curtains her mother had ordered from Spain, handling the banister where Suzy had broken a tooth when she was six. The thought made Pamela a little dizzy. She showed Mr. Harding out and began to wander through her house.

Briefly panic gripped her, and she thought desperately of calling for Philip. Just a word, she knew, and the house could be saved. But she would have to pay the price with the rest of her life.

She looked up at the portrait of her grandfather hanging over the living-room mantel. Did he understand? Would he forgive her?

She had a cold feeling that he would do no such thing. Maybe she should marry Philip. What would it hurt? He'd be good and kind. She knew that. But she could never love him.

Too old for love. That was what Suzy thought. Pamela stopped before the mirror in the hall and looked at her face. Still attractive, but so careworn. Had she ever been young?

Yes, once. It seemed so long ago now. But once she'd skipped down this very hall with nothing more on her mind than meeting her friends for pizza or the Saturday-night dance.

She'd had a normal, happy childhood. She'd laughed and cried and grown up the same way everyone else had. She'd loved her parents without reservation. Even if she'd understood then that her father was gambling away all their money, she'd have loved him just as much. But she'd probably been happier not knowing.

She'd gone away to college in Oregon. Her mother had died during her senior year, but despite her grief she'd finished school and taken a job in Sacramento as legislative assistant to a state senator. The work had engrossed her and she'd made fewer and fewer trips home, leaving her father to raise Suzy on his own.

Thinking about it now brought an overpowering wave of guilt. How could she have been so selfish all those years? If only she'd come home more often, she might have seen...might have been able to prevent...

Her final homecoming, a little more than a year before, had been a horrifying, tear-stained drive in the night after a hysterical call from Suzy. Their father had shot himself to death in the garage. Now all they had was each other.

She'd resigned her post in Sacramento and stayed at White Acres while Suzy finished high school. Soon the long white envelopes began to come in the mail. And there were phone calls from creditors clamoring for their money. She'd turned in desperation to Mr. Harding, who had been her grandfather's financial adviser. Her father had dismissed him. She realized too late that he'd wanted no one looking over his shoulder while he gambled away every cent the family had, plus quite a bit more than they ever hoped to see.

Mr. Harding was a rock. He'd tried, twisting everything this way and that, to find a way out of the maze of debts, and he had made quite a bit of progress. But after a year of shuffling the cards, they had to admit the truth. White Acres would have to be sold to pay off years of back taxes.

They'd waited as long as they could. But now Suzy was through school, and they were free to leave the area. The inevitable couldn't be postponed any longer.

The sharp ring of the telephone broke into her reverie.

"Pamela, darling." It was Bernice. "Did you do it? Did you sign away your mother's house to that awful man?"

Bernice tended toward the dramatic. Despite her mood, Pamela smiled at her friend's tone. "Mr. Harding is hardly the villain twirling a mustache. And I'm not exactly poor pitiful Pauline. You make it sound as though he'd tied me to the railroad track."

"He might as well have!" Bernice sighed. "I can't imagine how you can let White Acres go to strangers. The valley won't be the same without you here."

"Nothing stays the same, Bernice. That's one of the hardest lessons in life, but we all have to face it sometime." She hoped she didn't sound too bitter.

"My, aren't we philosophical." Bernice didn't seem to appreciate her little homily wisdom or the stoicism behind it. "I just called to tell you not to take the first offer that comes along. When it comes in, give it some time to simmer. And let me know! Okay?"

Pamela hesitated suspiciously. "Why?"

"Just do it. Promise me?"

Pamela shook her head, a slight smile on her lips. "This wouldn't have anything to do with Philip, would it?"

"Well, why not?" Bernice gave an exasperated sniff. "He deserves one last chance at changing your mind."

Every one of her friends thought she was crazy to reject Philip's proposal. He was the wealthiest, most successful landowner in the valley now, and they all respected him.

"He may not be the most exciting man around," Bernice had counseled her more than once, "but you'll know where he is at night. And believe me, that's worth a lot."

Bernice herself had already been through a nasty divorce from a husband who'd spent many a night away from her bed. Now she was involved with Fred Parsons, a quiet dairy farmer. This time, she assured everyone who would listen, she was betting on security over flash.

Bernice was ready to discuss everyone who'd been at the party the day before, cataloging each outfit and speculating on relationships. But Pamela hadn't the patience for gossip today. She felt a restlessness, a need to escape.

She ended the conversation with Bernice as gently as possible, then wandered out into the yard. She knew what was drawing her, and she tried to resist it. But she found herself walking faster and faster, until she came to the small, overgrown plot among the peppertrees that had once served as the family burial ground. The bodies had been moved to the county cemetery decades ago, but the old headstones remained. Weeds grew around them, but bending down, Pamela could run her fingers over the old letters and read the names once again as she had done so often as a child.

"Sarah Winston Starbuck, 1875-1932." "Ishmael Grant Starbuck, 1835-1899." "Merrick Wentworth Starbuck, 1845-1863."

The history of her family was there. Pioneers who came across the plains in covered wagons, searching for gold, searching for a better life. A soldier who died from Civil War wounds. A mother who died in childbirth. A preacher; a farmer; wives and helpmates. Their blood ran in her veins. Their dreams still stirred in her heart. How could she forsake them this way?

Huge, racking sobs tore at her throat and she gave in to them, crying out loud, letting the anguish wash through her, hoping it would wash away the guilt and shame.

It didn't do that. It did leave her feeling exhausted and empty. She rose, walked slowly back to the house and bathed her face in cool water. She examined her reflection in the mirror, noting how hollow her cheeks seemed, how haunted her eyes looked, with the dark circles below them. She remembered how her father had once called her his apple-cheeked girl. That had been when she was younger, before she'd known she was living a life of false appearances.

Apple-cheeked. Yes, she'd been that. Smiling and rosy and always laughing. How long had it been since she'd laughed, really laughed? The only time she could think of was yesterday, with Michael Donovan.

She went into her bedroom and walked to the window, staring at the acres of green that spread out from the house. She looked at the swing, the horse trails, the orchard trees full of dazzling pink and white blossoms, and everything she saw pained her. It hurt to look at all the beloved things she was so soon to lose.

There was only one thought that didn't hurt. She let her mind float back to visions of Michael Donovan, and a small smile etched itself on her tired face. Suddenly she made up her mind. Turning to her closet, she quickly changed into white slacks and a plaid shirt. She braided her burnished hair, letting the two plaits hang on either side of her head, and put on sneakers. Then she ran outside before she could think about what she was planning or let her better judgment stop her.

The river was half a mile from the house. She often heard its roar on spring nights, when it was swollen by the runoff from the snow in the mountains. She listened for it as she walked through the spring grass, past the stables, which had been empty now for more than a year. Then she headed into the stand of black oaks that lined the edge of the meadow.

It had been years since she'd taken this path to the river. With a lighter heart she remembered all those hot summer days when she and her friends had found one reason or another to go for a hike along the banks. Once she'd known the area as well as she knew the floorplan of her own house. Walking into the familiar shadows, she felt as though she were being welcomed back.

The water tumbled and splashed against the rocks, just as she remembered. She knew it was ice-cold. Only a short time earlier, it had been part of the snow cover that still coated the slopes of the Sierra, even though summer was coming. Now it was part of the runoff that surged through the foothills as that snow melted. Soon it would be part of the eternal sea.

But this river carried a secret on its way to the sea. Crashing through the granite crevices of the mountains, the water often scooped up bits and pieces of shattered gold veins and carried the heavy mineral as long as it could. That was what drew men to the river, what had drawn the Indians for hundreds of years, and what drew the exploring Spaniards with their dreams of golden cities. It drew the forty-niners who came swarming into California during the Gold Rush. And even these days, it drew the occasional prospector.

Pamela moved swiftly, jumping from one rock to another, toward the sandy bar where most river people set up camp. She knew why she was going there, though she wouldn't let herself think too much about the reason. Michael Donovan had comforted her the day before. Now she felt an aching need for more of that comfort.

There was just one large, uprooted ponderosa pine between her and the sandbar. She negotiated her way around the huge trunk, turned back toward the river and rounded the boulder at the edge of the bar, heart beating quickly, expecting to see Michael's tent. There was nothing but empty, windswept beach. She had difficulty taking it in for a moment. She'd been so sure...

Her heart fell, and a wave of disappointment curled through her. He wasn't there. Either he'd already gone, or he'd never camped there in the first place. He was gone, and with him, her hope.

Hope for what? She wasn't sure. But he'd said he'd take care of her wishes, hadn't he? Irrationally she felt angry with him for letting her down.

She picked up a rounded stone and threw it into the river, then turned upstream, heading for a road that would be an easier route home than the way she'd come. She was fuming inside, at Michael Donovan for deserting her, and at herself for being such a fool.

Who was he, after all? Just some river pirate, a passerby. A tramp, Philip had called him. And Philip was right. Michael Donovan had seen her standing on the hill in her white dress and she had intrigued him. He'd climbed up, had some fun at her expense and left again. That was all. Why on earth had she thought he might want to continue such a meaningless encounter? She must be losing her mind!

She decided she'd been lucky not to find him after all. What would be have thought of her? A little harmless flirtation, and the woman follows him home like a lost puppy. She blushed just thinking about it. No, it was better this way. She'd tried to escape, but there was nowhere to hide. She had to go back and face what was happening to her life, to her family. This little dash for freedom had been a momentary illusion.

She came to the place where the river cut into the alluvial plain. She began to climb up the bank, which rose steeply above the water, forming a cliff. The brush was thick and as she pushed her way through it, she saw a flash of something at the river below. Looking down, she saw him.

She froze, one hand in the midst of pushing aside a branch. There he was, in the shallow water at the edge of the river. He'd rigged up a simple sluice, and was scooping dirt from the riverbed and sifting through it, looking for gold, just as she'd originally surmised.

She couldn't see him very well. The bushes blocked her view. Moving slowly so as not to attract his attention, she worked her way farther upriver and found a place at the edge of the cliff where she could get a clear view. Then she knelt behind a bush and peered down at him.

He couldn't have heard her. The roar of the river was much too loud. Even if she shouted he might not catch the sound at first.

And he hadn't seen her. He was much too intent on his work to notice her passing above him. She could run away without his ever knowing that she'd come looking for him.

That was very important now. It had been one thing to run thoughtlessly through the woods looking for a balm to her spirit, it was quite another to sashay into the wilderness searching for a man as dangerous as Michael Donovan.

For dangerous was just what he seemed to her now. She watched as he bent over his wooden riggings, reaching into the water in the sluice, sifting through the silt and sand, hoping to catch a flicker of gold among the dross. He'd taken off his shirt and his well-muscled body shone slick and wet in the late-morning sun. As he worked, those muscles seemed to smooth and then tighten in a rhythmic, hypnotic way, and she found herself staring, fascinated.

His chest was broad and coated with a mat of curling dark hair that tapered to a point at his navel. He wore his jeans low on his hips, revealing more muscles blending together in a supple show of strength that quite suddenly took her breath away.

She sat back, stunned. Here she was, looking at a man's body in a way she'd never done before, and it was definitely affecting her! Yes, dangerous was the word for Michael Donovan. Too dangerous for a sane and sensible woman like Pamela. She bit her lip, leaning forward again to watch, knowing she would have to leave, but guiltily reluctant to take the first step.

He was looking straight toward her, his hand shielding his eyes from the sun. She sat very still, her heart beating in her throat, fear prickling along her spine, caught like a deer in a clearing. Then he looked away and bent again to his work. With a shudder of relief, she realized he hadn't seen her, after all.

But at least her fright gave her the impetus she needed to speed her on her way. Backing from her hiding spot, she turned to run along the path to the road that led away from the river. She'd hardly taken three steps before a sound stopped her—a sound she could hear even over the roar of the river.

It was an engine sound. She shrank back into the bushes and peered out, but she couldn't see anything moving through the trees. The sound got louder and she looked up at the sky. There was a helicopter descending to the river with the grace of a giant dragonfly.

A helicopter. She'd never seen one on the river before. She watched, fascinated, as it came closer and closer. Just over the spot where she'd seen Michael Donovan, it stopped, blades beating the air into a small hurricane all around her. She protected her face from the flailing branches but peered out between her fingers. The helicopter was lowering a ropelike ladder into the river canyon. And then she saw Michael climbing it.

He'd put a shirt on and his pack was slung across his back. She stood, wanting to shout to him, but she didn't, and he didn't see her. He was going away. A lump of disappointment filled her throat, but she also felt a soaring sense of excitement, of adventure. She watched as he pulled the ladder in after himself. And then the helicopter was careering up the canyon, heading for the clouds.

He was gone. She emerged from the brush and began walking slowly homeward. Michael Donovan was special. There was magic about him. She hadn't needed to see him fly off into the sky to tell her that.

But it helped. She smiled, stripping the leaves from a branch as she passed. It certainly helped.

She was going back to face a bleak, uncertain future. Could Michael have saved her? Of course not. No one could do that. *But still*, a small part of her whispered rebelliously, *still, he might have done something*. She should have let him try.

CHAPTER THREE

"OH, GO TO PHILIP'S PARTY," Suzy told her older sister impatiently, her fist full of weeds she'd just uprooted from the edge of the tiny backyard garden. "You've been in mourning for White Acres long enough. It'll do you good to get out and have a little fun."

Pamela leaned back against the frayed plastic ribbing of the lawn chair and sighed, shading her eyes against the low autumn sun. The two of them had been spending Saturday afternoon sprucing up the yard of their new residence. "I wasn't formally invited, you know," she mused. "In fact, I almost got the feeling Philip didn't really want me to come." A sly smile curled her lips. "What if I went and he had another date with him?"

Suzy laughed, throwing the weeds into the small compost heap and pulling off the rubber gloves she'd worn to protect her hands. "It would do you both good," she chortled. "Shake up the relationship a little, get some blood into it. You two act like Victorian lovers watching each other from behind fans or something."

The word *lovers* brought to mind a face Pamela hadn't thought of in weeks. Michael Donovan. What had ever happened to him, she wondered. She'd thought about him almost constantly for a while, at the height of the summer, when things were going very badly for her and Suzy. She'd found herself thinking of him as some sort of savior, thinking "If only Michael Donovan were here, things would be different."

How silly, really. She'd met him for only a few moments on a windswept hill, then watched him being whisked away in a rather spectacular manner, and his image had stayed with her for months after. "You're just building an impossible dream in your mind," she'd scolded herself more than once. "He's just a man. Nothing more. He couldn't do anything to help you, even if he were here."

But some perverse part of her had clung to the picture of him climbing the rope ladder to the helicopter. A sort of sensitive Superman. Her dream lover. The only man...well, that was enough of that silliness. Suzy had called Philip her lover in jest, and that was all it could ever be.

"We're not lovers, at all," Pamela reminded her. "And we never will be."

"I know, I know." Suzy shook her golden hair. "I only wanted that when I was desperate to save White Acres."

They'd left White Acres in the middle of summer, tears blinding them both. The papers had been signed, the closets and shelves swept clean of all their possessions. Their land had been bought by a company called Miracle Development, and Pamela didn't dare speculate what they might want with her home. She'd asked Mr. Harding if they could attach a proviso to the sale outlawing certain things—like condominiums or circus tents. Mr. Harding had been sad but firm. She would have absolutely no control over what happened to White Acres once it was sold. She still tried not to think about what might be going on there. She still avoided driving by and avoided speaking to anyone who might know. She needed time to adjust to the way things were.

But they'd lived through the change, paying off the debts and buying a small shop with an apartment above it in town. That was how they made their living now, selling local handiworks and artifacts in the store they were slowly renovating.

In fact, Pamela had to admit to a certain satisfaction with her new life. It was only when her mind turned to the green fields of White Acres that she felt the stone in the pit of her stomach, the ache in her heart. But that life was finished. Suzy was right. It was time to move on.

"Maybe I will go," she sighed, closing her eyes. "It's time I let the others know I'm ready to join the living again." She smiled. "And we could use a little more business. Maybe if I tell everyone about our shop—"

"Oh, not until we're ready," Suzy interrupted. She'd enjoyed working on the store as much as Pamela had. "I want everything to be perfect. Then I think we should have a grand opening. Don't you? With refreshments and everything."

Pamela nodded. "Yes, good idea." She glanced up at the mountains. "Would you like to come along?"

"To the party?"

Pamela smiled. "No, to the zoo. What else have we been talking about?"

Suzy didn't mind being twitted. "Then you're really going? Great! I'd love to come along."

"I'm sure it will be all right. I know Bernice is going, and so is just about everyone else we know."

But Pamela frowned, remembering. "Though Philip did seem strange when he mentioned it. I had the distinct impression he was relieved when I said I didn't think I could make it."

Suzy shrugged. "He was probably just sparing your feelings." She said the last three words with exaggerated drama. "He'll be thrilled to see you."

Pamela smiled. "Maybe I should call him..."

"No," Suzy insisted, bounding up from her seat. "Surprise him! That will be so much more fun."

Later, Pamela realized she'd only got what she deserved for listening to a teenager's advice instead of following her own conscience. But at the time, it seemed the easiest thing to do. Besides, she was sure Suzy was right. Philip would be thrilled.

He didn't look very thrilled when she arrived. Nor did anyone else. As she glanced around, she realized that every pair of eyes she met was registering some degree of consternation. But by the time that realization had sunk in, she was caught up in a whirl of greetings and didn't have time to explore it fully.

"Pamela, my dear," Philip said, a tiny frown between his brows, as he hurried toward them. "I'm so...glad you could make it, after all." He looked around, almost at a loss, and grabbed the first available arm. "Do you remember Pamela Starbuck?" he demanded. "Here she is."

She'd worn a red wool knit with a stand-up collar and black buttons. It was a striking outfit and she'd hesitated at first, wondering if she would be overdressed, then decided to wear it, anyway, because she needed the ego boost. The dress skimmed her slim body perfectly and she knew she looked good.

Observing the others around her, she realized she hadn't overdone it at all. The standard of dress was almost formal. People she usually saw in overalls and cowboy boots were slicked down and dressed to the nines. She wondered with a slight smile whom they were all trying to impress.

"So nice to meet you," she murmured again and again. The room was filled with strangers, as well as the usual crowd. But what surprised her was the number of town notables present—the mayor, the members of the city council, the president of the major bank. Philip did business with them all, she knew, but she didn't think she'd ever been to a party where every one of them had shown up. Some were barely on speaking terms, if the stories she'd heard were true. And yet here they all were, smiling and offering toasts to one another. What was going on?

Suzy had disappeared the minute they'd come in the door, looking for others of her own age. She'd dressed herself with delighted anticipation of the effect she'd have, wearing a shift that looked as if it had come from a Martian rummage sale and teasing her hair into spikes. "Too rad," she'd pronounced after an admiring look in the mirror.

"Too bad," Pamela had responded, shaking her head with rueful amusement at her sister's idea of great style.

So when they'd arrived, Suzy had been anxious to show off her trendy style to someone who could appreciate it. Now she was back, looking lonely. "I shouldn't have come," she whispered to her sister. "It's a party for dinosaurs!"

"Pamela, darling!" Bernice had spotted them at last. She rushed at Pamela and kissed her hastily. "I'm so glad you're out again, but why now, darling, why here?"

"You're right," Suzy announced enthusiastically. "Let's go home."

Bernice shifted her attention to Suzy before Pamela had time to respond. "Oh, I love it!" she cried, motioning for Suzy to turn slowly. "That darling dress! The hairstyle! Did Maurice do that for you? I'm going to ask him to do the same for me next week."

Suzy rolled her eyes. "What's the use of being outrageous," she moaned, "if no one's outraged?"

"Who could be outraged by such fashion sense?" Bernice asked airily. "You must meet my nephew Jeremy. He's just moved to town from San Francisco. He dropped out of Berkeley and wants to 'learn to live with nature' or some such nonsense. You'll love him."

"Is he cute?" Suzy asked hopefully.

"Adorable," responded his proud aunt.

Pamela ignored their exchange. She'd caught the strange tone of Bernice's original question, and she wanted an explanation.

"What did you mean, Bernice?" she asked sharply. "Why shouldn't I have come now, and here?"

Bernice opened her mouth, then closed it again, avoiding her friend's eyes. "Didn't anyone tell you?" she asked, suddenly uncomfortable.

"No," Pamela said. "Why don't you tell me?"

But just as she finished her sentence, her gaze swept the room, and suddenly the answer didn't matter anymore. Nothing mattered. Nothing but the man who'd seen her at the same moment she'd seen him.

Michael Donovan. Strangely she didn't wonder how he'd got there, or why. It felt as though he'd come for her, as though he'd been waiting for this moment. She had no doubt that he wanted to see her as much as she wanted to see him.

She vaguely remembered some song heard often when she was a child, something about strangers' eyes meeting across a crowded room, about magic and souls touching and the rest of the world fading away. And that was exactly how it happened.

His blue eyes held hers and though he didn't smile, he didn't need to. She started toward him, leaving Suzy and Bernice behind as though she'd forgotten they existed. And he started toward her, weaving his way among chatting people, not even glancing at those who tried to detain him. All the while, their gazes never wavered. And finally they met, standing still, not touching, not saying a word. He put out an arm. She slipped her hand into the crook of his elbow. He led her out of the room through the open French doors, onto the patio where they could be alone.

"Hello," he said softly, looking down into her eyes.

"Hello," she answered, smiling up.

"I knew I'd find you again," he said.

"Yes," she answered. "So did I."

Someone seemed to be calling to them from the house but Pamela didn't look to see who it was, and Michael didn't, either. He waved an acknowledging hand, but took her elbow and steered her out into the gardens, away from prying eyes.

Philip's gardens were well kept and formal. They were set away from the house, different sections separated by rows of trees, all meeting around a central fountain. Certain sections were visible from the house, others were hidden by the trees.

"No wishing well," Michael said regretfully, glancing about at the roses and the fountain, which was in the form of a leaping dolphin spouting water in all directions.

No need for one now, Pamela thought, but she wasn't quite brave enough to say it aloud. She left him instead, dropping his arm and walking forward to trail her fingers in the silvery water of the fountain. "You look so different," she said gazing back at him over her shoulder. "I thought you were a river rat. A gold miner."

"I am," he replied, coming to stand beside her. "This is all a sham, a disguise." He gestured toward the charcoal-gray suit that fitted him as though he'd flown to Paris and had it sewn to his body. "At heart I belong on the river with a gold pan in my hands."

She smiled at him. The evening shadows were lengthening, and his blue eyes caught the reflection of the last of the sunlight. She could reach out and touch him, and she knew she soon would. But for now, she savored the pull, the excitement between them, the spark that seemed to flare whenever their gazes met.

He was even more handsome than she'd remembered. From his jet-black hair to his finely chiseled chin, he was a masterpiece of masculinity, yet there was a warmth in his gaze, a hidden twinkle only glimpsed now and again.

She threw back her head and searched the blue mystery of his eyes. "Did you find your fortune in my river?" she finally asked, forgetting that the river was no longer hers, that it had never really been hers at all.

His gaze skimmed across the planes of her face as though he was trying to memorize each angle. "I found more than I ever dreamed of," he replied softly, touching her cheek with the edge of his hand. "Much more." His smile muted the intensity of his statement. Taking her arm, he began their walk again. "And I also found some nice gold nuggets."

She didn't analyze what he'd said, didn't try to decide if he might be teasing or flirting. She was drifting again, just as she had the first time they'd met. This wasn't reality. It was a dream, so facts and motives didn't matter. She was free to delight in it, to take with gratitude whatever she was given.

"You struck it rich then."

"Oh yes." He halted near a gardenia bush and, gently disengaging her arm, began to pull blossoms from among the satiny green leaves. "And now I've come back to claim my prize," he continued without looking at her.

"Have you?" She laughed softly. "You've waited quite a long time, haven't you?"

He broke off a long frond of asparagus fern and carefully wove it through the gardenia stems. "The finest wine grows richer with anticipation," he murmured, frowning at his work, applying a tug here, a pinch there, then turning toward her with a garland as nearly perfect as any she'd ever seen. "Do you like it?" he asked.

She nodded, dark eyes shining, and he placed it on the crown of her head, nestling it among the auburn curls. "Where did you learn to do that?" she asked, delighted.

He put a finger to his lips and glanced around as though making sure they weren't overheard. "An old leprechaun taught me," he whispered. "He gave me other powers, too."

She couldn't resist a smile to match the one in his eyes. "Did he?"

He nodded his dark head. "Yes. He taught me to see into the future," he said, taking her hand, his gaze holding hers. "I'm looking there right now."

She felt as though she were staring into a pool of sparkling water, anticipating a plunge. "And what do you see?" she asked breathlessly.

His grin was wide and inviting. "That depends. Are you more interested in the far distant future—" he drew her toward him, his breath teasing her skin "—or something much closer?"

Her heart was pounding fiercely and she felt light-headed. "Right now, I think the close one is all I can take."

"Good," he murmured huskily, leaning closer. "That's what I'm interested in, too."

His eyes had deepened to a blue that was almost black. A delicious trembling was beginning in the pit of her stomach. His hands cupped her face as she lifted her eyes to meet his.

"Here it is," he whispered. "A prophecy—and a promise."

His kiss was so gentle that if she hadn't been watching, she might have thought she'd dreamt it. His lips were soft and smooth and they slipped across hers as lightly as the breeze might rustle a daffodil on a spring day. But then she closed her eyes and parted her lips, yielding to his caress, and his mouth hardened with a new purpose, hardened the way a panther might set his muscles before a strike, still slick and smooth as velvet, but sure and strong and fine.

Pamela realized dimly, that she'd never really been kissed before. Oh, she'd had her share of dates and even thought she had been in love once, for about three days when she was nineteen. And she'd been kissed and snuggled and had men try to seduce her. But she'd never had the slightest trouble turning a man down. There'd been no spark, no compulsion to continue. She'd always known where to draw the line and had never been tempted to drop her barriers.

But that was probably because she'd never really been kissed before.

She knew that now, because she *was* being kissed, and it was so far removed from those other shallow, groping encounters, it might have come from another galaxy. Galactic, that was exactly what it was like. As though a new, limitless horizon had opened before her, and she was shooting through it on the back of a comet, bound for a star-studded sky.

His mouth on hers was sweet persuasion, hot and tingling, smooth and secure. She felt his hand slip around to take hold of the back of her head, fingers raking into her hair, and she arched toward him, wanting to feel his body against hers. His other hand was between her shoulder blades, pressing her to his chest, and she gasped as the bottom of her stomach seemed to drop away.

The sense of his maleness was overpoweringly seductive. When she felt him slacken his hold she heard a small moan and realized, to her horror, that it was her own sound of regret.

Still embracing her, he smiled down into her face, then lightly brushed a feather of hair from her eyes while she stared up at him in wonder.

"Why did you come back?" she asked, her voice slurred, her eyelids heavy.

"To find you."

She searched his gaze, then laughed, half believing him, wanting to believe him. She gave her head a slight shake, trying to clear it. "I wasn't aware that I was lost."

"Ah, but you were." He smiled. "Lost to me. Until the time was right."

"Is it right now?"

His shrug was barely perceptible beneath his silk jacket. "I hope so."

She hoped so, too. Oh, how she hoped! She'd never known a man like this before. From the first, she'd been aware that he was different and that she was fascinated by those differences. She'd hungered for his kiss without even realizing it. Now she knew. He was the only man she'd ever met who could make her fall in love. She wondered if he understood this.

He reached out to straighten the garland on her head, and then they were laughing together, neither of them knowing quite why. The sun had dipped below the horizon, and dusk was gathering all around them. The scent of gardenias filled the air. The only sounds were the splash of the fountain and the laughter of lovers. Arm in arm, they walked through the gardens, whispering, laughing, stealing an occasional kiss. They were suspended in time, living a dream.

"Come with me," Michael said at last, flicking her hair behind her ear with his forefinger.

"Where?" she asked, not really caring, ready to go wherever he might lead her.

"Away from here." He took her chin in his hand and gazed down into her eyes, his own deep with meaning. "Somewhere we can be alone. Completely alone."

"Completely alone," she echoed. She knew what he meant, and she knew that she wanted it, too. She raised her hand to stroke his cheek. "I'll go with you," she whispered, still caught in the dream. "Anywhere."

His lips touched hers in a quick salute. And then, suddenly, there were people coming out from the house, pulling them back to reality. Pamela resisted like a drowsy girl craving just one more moment of sleep, but it was too late. People were coming toward them, shouting their names, dispelling the dream.

Michael seemed to feel the same way. He moved between her and the light from the house, as though trying to shield her from Philip, who called in a disgruntled voice, "Donovan, we've waited as long as we can. We're going to have to get started."

"Not now," Michael replied, and his tone should have settled things then and there, but Suzy and Bernice had rushed forward and all became confusion.

"Pamela!" Suzy snapped, peering through the shadows. "You won't believe what they're up to. You've got to see the horrible thing they've done."

"Oh, darling, I knew it wasn't wise for you to be here," Bernice broke in, bending back branches to get a better view. "Why don't you let me take you home...."

Their voices reminded her of the way the others had greeted her earlier, and suddenly she knew what she should have guessed before. This had something to do with Michael. She turned to look at him questioningly, ready to let his arms enfold her, hoping he would tell her not to worry, but the look on his face stopped her cold.

"Pamela..." he began, but she stepped back quickly, avoiding the hand he was holding out to her.

"What's going on?" she asked, now very calm, very rational. The dream had completely faded away.

Philip's face was crinkled with concern. "I...I wish you'd let me know you were planning to come, Pamela," he said sorrowfully. "It really would be best if you let Bernice take you home..."

"I'm perfectly capable of taking myself home." She looked from one pair of anxious eyes to another. "Now tell me what this is all about."

Everyone looked at Michael. Pamela turned to look at him too. He stared at her for a moment, and grimaced in exasperation. "Come on, then. Why don't you see for yourself?" he said roughly.

CHAPTER FOUR

SHE KNEW that it must have something to do with White Acres, but she didn't want to speculate, so she kept her mind blank, smiling at friends she passed on her way back to the house. She walked between Bernice on one side and Suzy on the other, effectively cutting off Michael. She didn't want him to touch her just then, and he seemed to accept that. He was immediately engulfed by others who each wanted a word with him.

Most of the people at the party seemed to have moved outside, waiting to see what she and Michael were up to. They lined the walkway, holding drinks and craning their necks, enjoying the parade. Despite the tension, or perhaps because of it, Pamela almost laughed aloud. A strange giddiness had infected her. She felt apart, a little separate from the others, as though she were an observer. As though nothing could touch her.

"Where is the awful thing you want me to see?" she asked Suzy as they entered the house.

"It's about White Acres," Suzy whispered, and Pamela nodded. "Show her, Jeremy," Suzy said, and for the first time, Pamela noticed the rail-thin, intense-looking young man in a plaid shirt who was walking at Suzy's other side. Bernice's nephew, she deduced, her mind curiously sharp on extraneous details.

"I don't know if you should do that," Bernice was saying, waving vaguely toward the front door as though trying to shoo Pamela in that direction. But Pamela wasn't about to leave.

"Show me, Jeremy," she said. She felt calm, so calm.

"This way." The young man led her into the study where a table had been set up. One side was piled high with slickly produced leaflets and brochures. The other held a large scale model of a landscape molded in plasticene and painted with brightly realistic colors. It was White Acres, all right. White Acres covered with buildings that had never been there before.

"They're turning it into some sort of resort," Suzy explained. "Look, see the hotel rooms they're planning? And the new stables right on top of the old cemetery. The golf course? They're going to cut down all the forest along one side of the river. So that the tourists can have a better view from their rooms, they say. And they're putting in a dock for river rafting."

Pamela nodded and didn't say a word. The strange calm still gripped her. Her eyes flickered over the model, taking in everything.

The room was filling with people. Philip approached the table, sent an apologetic glance her way and called for attention.

"I'm sure you all know why you were invited here," he began, and Bernice tugged at her sleeve.

"Let me take you home," she whispered, but Pamela shook her head. She felt the gardenias slip and she reached up to take the garland from her head, clutching it tightly in her fingers. She stepped back so that she could watch Philip speak. She didn't once look at Michael, who stood across the room from her, waiting, as though expecting to speak himself.

"White Acres," Philip was saying, "has been a fixture in our little valley since the first pioneers wandered through our green hills following their fortunes. I know I speak for every one of us when I say how sorry we all were when the Starbuck family was forced to give up this wonderful piece of land." He nodded deferentially toward Pamela and she lifted her chin a shade higher, blinking quickly as the others in the room murmured their agreement. "I, for one, was sickened at the thought of strangers coming in, turning White Acres into a housing development or a shopping mall." He shuddered visibly, and all the others seemed to shudder along with him. "Luckily the purchaser was Miracle Development. Oh, just like you, I worried at first. But we've got to move with the times, you know. And when I went over and got firsthand look at what this fine company was doing, I became a firm supporter. There are changes going on, big changes, and I think you'll agree with me that they will make our valley prosper as it never has before." He glanced at Pamela, seemed to lose his place, then cleared his throat and went on.

"I invited you all here today to meet the man behind these changes. Miracle Development is a privately owned company. Marshall Bentworth started it forty years ago, and he is still the titular head. Today it's being run by Michael Donovan, his stepson. Come on up here, Michael."

Marshall Bentworth. Pamela remembered the name. It had been on the papers she'd signed. She remembered deriving some hope from it at the time. The name had sounded staid and substantial. But now she knew the name really didn't mean a thing. Michael was obviously in charge of developing White Acres. Her Michael. The man she'd been falling in love with only moments before.

Michael was moving forward, a politician's smile on his face, an arrogant spring in his step, and Pamela cringed. This was what she'd been waiting for—and dreading.

But she should have known the truth from the moment she'd spotted him across the room, so finely dressed, so sure of himself. Her river pirate had turned out to be a different kind of pirate altogether, and she felt betrayed.

When he'd come to her on that windy hill, she'd thought he was a prospector. She'd talked and laughed and let him charm her, never realizing his motives. He'd been there to look over her land, to see if it was going to suit his purposes. And he'd hidden his real intentions. He hadn't lied in so many words, but he'd lied in spirit.

She stood watching him, a tense smile straining her lips, but she heard hardly a word he said. He was going on about jobs for the area, about national prestige and money for schools, but those weren't things that concerned her just then. She was thinking about White Acres being turned into an amusement park for rich tourists, about developers cashing in its fundamental worth and history for the cold change in a bored vacationer's pocket. About selling out. About losing one's lifeblood. About lies and deception.

She'd already lost White Acres. She knew that well enough. And she thought she'd mourned. But now she understood that her mourning was just beginning. She was about to lose White Acres all over again. The man she'd whimsically thought might save her was about to grind it under his heel.

What a fool she was. She'd been so thrilled to see him again, never bothering to wonder why he'd come. "I've come back to claim my prize," he'd said, and she'd assumed he meant her! Her mouth went dry and her cheeks felt flushed, but she kept the smile rigidly in place.

Michael was busy selling his project to the crowd. She wondered why he thought he needed to do that. For community support? For money? Or was he courting them for the same reason he'd courted her? Whatever his motive, he was a born salesman, and she was sure he'd win them over. He'd certainly sold her a bill of goods with very little effort.

Suddenly a voice from the group broke into her thoughts. "I'd like to hear what Miss Starbuck thinks of this," somebody was saying, and everyone turned to her, including Michael.

She stepped forward, still calm, though trembling slightly. She looked around the room at all the faces, many of them familiar. "It sounds wonderful, doesn't it?" she said at last. "Acapulco on the banks of our own Crater River." Her smile was brittle. "Now I suppose we'll find out how the people who sold Mr. Disney the property for his amusement park must have felt when it turned out to be the number-one tourist attraction in the world." She paused and then said significantly, "It's a nice place to visit, but you wouldn't want to live there."

A murmur swept through the room and she turned, still smiling, to Michael. "Good evening, Mr. Donovan," she said.

Inclining his head in a slight nod, he didn't reply. His eyes were cold as an Arctic sea. She could hardly believe this was the same gaze that had warmed her very soul only a short time before. He didn't like what she'd done. She tossed her head as she turned to go. That made them even. She didn't like what he'd done. She didn't like it at all.

"WELL, ONE GOOD THING about Michael Donovan's resort," Suzy said the next morning as they were dusting the stock in their little store. "It should improve business for us. Who knows? Maybe we'll get rich."

"People who are interested in getting rich don't come to live in our valley," Pamela replied caustically. "Those who live here come for peace and quiet and to get away from people in a hurry to get rich."

"Only kidding," Suzy said in a tiny voice that made Pamela ashamed of her outburst.

"Oh, honey, I didn't mean to snap at you." She hugged her sister before returning to her work. She seemed to be full of energy today, nervous energy that needed constant outlet. First she straightened the shelf of fancy candles, made in the shape of various forest creatures by Jerry Renault, who lived in a cabin along the river. Then she turned to the rack of delicate brass earrings made by Betsy Clark, the town's assistant sheriff. She decided the display looked untidy, so she took every pair down and began to hang them all over again.

She'd been moving about like a crazed robot ever since the previous evening. Even after falling asleep, she'd found herself jerking awake, her mind running at double speed. Her emotions had been anesthetized, she decided. Her body wouldn't let her slow down and face things. Not yet.

Bernice had tried to drive her home, which she had refused. Philip had hovered about solicitously, but she wanted nothing from him. He was a traitor. She pressed her lips together and closed her eyes.

She knew she was being irrational, but she couldn't help it. She'd sold White Acres. It wasn't hers any longer. She had no say in what was done with it. She could have her opinion like everybody else, but there was nothing she could do to alter the course of its destiny. She had no right to any claim, even emotional. And yet...and yet...

White Acres would always be part of her. Nothing could tear it loose. And Michael Donovan taking her beloved home and turning it into an amusement park broke her heart. That was how she felt. She couldn't help it.

When the telephone rang and Suzy answered it, saying, "Oh, hello, Philip," and looking up, she shook her head. But Suzy covered the mouthpiece and whispered, "You'll have to talk to him sometime," and she knew her sister was right.

"Philip," she said evenly into the receiver. "What a surprise."

Sarcasm was wasted on him. "I wanted to find out how you were this morning. I feel terrible about what happened last night. That was no way for you to find out about it. I meant to—"

Philip wasn't too perceptive, but she was wrong to blame him. "It's all right, Philip," she broke in reassuringly. "I'm an adult. I can handle it."

"But once you see what Miracle Development can do for this community," he went on, as though she hadn't said anything, "I'm sure you'll join me in singing their praises...."

That was carrying things a little too far, and Pamela wasn't ready to contemplate any such thing. "Philip," she said reproachfully, "I'm working right now. Perhaps we could talk later."

"I thought I might drop over," he suggested hopefully.

"No," she said quickly. "Not today."

She looked up gratefully at the jangling of the bell. Bernice's nephew, Jeremy, was entering the store. "Here's a customer," she told Philip. "I must go."

She laid the receiver gently in its cradle, watching with amusement as Jeremy and Suzy greeted each other. She hadn't realized the night before that the two of them had taken to each other so thoroughly. He was a nice-looking young man, if a little shaggy. As he entered the shop, his gaze swept the room somewhat anxiously. When he saw Suzy, the satisfied gleam in his eyes revealed just how pretty he thought she was.

And Pamela had to admit that Suzy was glowing as she watched Jeremy coming toward her. To Pamela, they seemed like two stars joining the same orbit—irresistibly attracted, each in awe of the other's brilliance.

Was that what she and Michael had looked like the night before? The thought came to her with a sudden violence and she wanted to shut it out, deny it. He'd made a fool of her. A man she'd thought she was falling in love with. She wasn't sure why he'd done it, but she was certain he wasn't going to get close enough to do it again.

"Hi," Jeremy greeted her when she joined them by the cash register. "Listen, I've been thinking about your problem."

She knew he meant what had happened the night before and she looked down at the knickknacks on the counter, smiling slightly. "It's nothing for you to worry about," she said softly.

"Oh, but it is," he retorted. "I've got all sorts of contacts with groups who've fought things like this. We just might be able to help you."

"Help me?" She looked at him curiously. "Help me to do what? I've sold the land. I can't do anything about the new owner's plans."

"You'd be surprised." He grinned and lifted his eyebrows suggestively. "It's been done before."

Pamela frowned. "What are you talking about? Buying back the land?"

He shook his head. "There are other ways." He threw his arms wide. "The legal system. The courts. The power of public opinion." He grinned again. "I'm working on it. I'll let you know what I come up with." Then he turned to Suzy and land problems faded. Pamela had to hide a smile. She thought she finally knew what the word *smitten* was all about.

"Jeremy's asked me to go on a picnic lunch with him," Suzy was saying tentatively. "I told him we were too busy...."

"Nonsense," Pamela told her. "You go on and have fun. Everyone gets a lunch hour, you know, even in sweatshops."

She was rewarded by a sparkling smile of happiness. But as she took Jeremy's arm, Suzy hesitated again. "You sure you'll be all right?" she asked her big sister, her eyes wide and anxious.

"Of course I'll be all right," Pamela replied, a bit startled. When had the positions been reversed, she wondered as she watched them walk out the door. When had Suzy begun to assume the role of caretaker? She shook her head ruefully. She mustn't let that happen. She wasn't an emotional invalid, and she mustn't let Suzy think she was.

She spent the next hour drawing up a plan for the shop, trying to organize where each type of item would be best displayed, trying to decide what the focus should be. She was interrupted a few times by browsers, but no one bought anything. The fact brought it home. The place needed work. She would have to upgrade the merchandise if she was going to make her living here.

Sheree Craighton came in with a selection of the beautiful jewelry she made, hoping to persuade Pamela to buy some pieces for resale. Sheree was a goldsmith with a very individual vision. Her rings and necklaces looked unlike any Pamela had ever seen before, light and airy as gossamer, yet substantial as the earth the gold had come from. She loved them. But because of the price she couldn't imagine any of her customers buying them.

"Oh, Sheree," she cried as she slipped on a ring that looked like a butterfly perched on her finger, "where do you get your unique ideas?"

The slim, stolid woman shrugged. "They're not really ideas," she said tonelessly. "I just start working and it flows from my fingers."

Pamela smiled at her, feeling a flicker of envy at such simple talent. She and Sheree had gone to school together, and though they'd never been close friends, they shared a common past of living alongside the river. Sheree's parents had a small plot of land bordering White Acres. They farmed it, but just barely. Sheree had left the valley at the same time Pamela had, leaving to marry a mechanic in Fresno. She'd also only recently returned, bringing her husband, now crippled by arthritis, with her. Pamela knew what it must cost her to have to live with her parents again—how much she must need the independence of making some money of her own. She wished she could help her.

"These are just so lovely," she said, looking through the jewelry, postponing the moment she would have to tell Sheree she couldn't take them. The bell jangled, signaling another customer, and she glanced up, meeting Michael's bright blue gaze across the shop.

Her heart fell, and she looked away quickly. She wasn't ready yet! She hadn't prepared how she was going to act toward him. She wasn't even sure how she felt about him. She needed time to assimilate all that had happened, all that he had turned out to be. Why wasn't he like Philip, asking permission before he came to bother her?

But no. Michael didn't ask permission. She'd known that from the first, and if she were honest she would admit to herself that his casual arrogance was one of the things that attracted her. But she didn't want to be honest!

Forcing herself to return her attention to Sheree, she picked up a lacy bracelet. "How much were you planning to ask for these?" she asked, damning the slight tremor she could hear in her own voice. Her heart was beating very fast. It was almost as though she could feel where Michael was without looking at him. She knew he was wandering around the shop, examining things, waiting for her to finish.

Sheree named her price and, disappointed, Pamela shook her head. She knew it was no use. Her clientele was not in the market for luxury items. But she couldn't turn Sheree away with nothing.

"I'm afraid that's too expensive for our little inventory. But I tell you what," she said instead. "I'll take two of each on consignment." She met the stony gaze of the other woman. "That's the best I can do until I see what sort of response we get."

She knew Sheree was also disappointed, even though there was no change in her colorless eyes. Without saying a thing, Sheree began dividing her jewelry, choosing two rings, two bracelets, two necklaces to leave with Pamela. They both stared at the golden ornaments while she sorted them, and they both jumped when Michael's voice broke the silence.

"That's a stunning collection you've got there. Did you make them yourself?"

Sheree swung around her face reddening when she saw who it was. "Oh, Mr. Donovan..." she began, but he stopped her with his charming smile.

"Michael," he insisted. "Nice to see you again, Sheree." He held out his hand and she took it, still blushing.

"I like your work," he said again. "I hope you'll bring some samples by when we start stocking our gift shop at White Acres. I'm sure we'll be able to provide you with a good market."

Cold fury surged through Pamela. Of course he would be able to provide Sheree with a market for her expensive jewelry. He would soon be loading the valley with rich people from all over the country. Not only had he taken away her birthright and turned it into a cheap amusement park, now he was setting up competition to take away her customers! She seethed, watching him escort Sheree to the door, still charming her with every word and smile.

The facts, of course, belied her angry accusations. A playground for the rich was not going to be "cheap." And the customers he was bringing in would in no way affect her little shop, whether or not they bought from his. She knew that. But she didn't want facts. She wanted weapons.

The doorbell signaled Sheree's departure, and then Michael was back to face her, his eyes no longer cold as they had been the night before, but hooded and searching.

"Somehow I have a feeling it wouldn't be wise to tell you that you're beautiful when you're angry, would it?" he asked softly.

She took a deep breath. "Why don't you leave right now and preserve that nice picture?" she suggested sharply. "I get uglier as the anger grows."

He seized her wrist in his strong fingers. "Then let's nip it in the bud, shall we?"

Her gaze was inexorably caught in his. "It's too late for that," she told him. "Too late and too deeply rooted."

She didn't try to pull free. She knew he was much too strong for her. But she lifted her chin and glared at him, just to let him know that physical superiority had nothing to do with winning this fight.

"I know you think I'm the big bad developer who's out to destroy the land of your ancestors," he said with a note of sarcasm in his tone. "But I'm not, you know."

"Aren't you?" She wished his eyes weren't quite so stunningly blue. "Prove it."

His fingers moved, circling her wrist. "Come out to White Acres with me and I will."

She frowned, very much aware of how the idea tempted her. She wanted to believe him, wanted to be friends again. But there was even more at stake than the issue of what he planned to do with "her" land.

"Why didn't you tell me who you were from the first?" she asked stiffly. "Why did you let me think you were a wanderer?"

He didn't answer for a long moment, and that in itself was a bad sign. What was he doing, she wondered? Judging which answer would work best with her? Or deciding whether to tell her the truth? The ache in her heart deepened as she waited for him to speak.

"When I saw you on that hill," he said finally, "I wasn't thinking about anything but you. You seemed like some sort of gift from the gods, something special and magic. I wanted to be close to you, to bask in your glow." He dropped her wrist and shrugged, leaning back a bit to look at her. "I thought we shared a special moment. It didn't occur to me at the time that you might want references."

"You were spying," she accused.

He shoved his hands into the pockets of his jeans and rocked back on his heels. "I'd call it scouting out the territory."

The coldness was creeping into his eyes again, and sent a chill to her heart. She desperately wanted to say something to end that look of bitter indifference, to restore the warmth. But she couldn't. Not yet. He had to explain. He had to wipe away this suspicion that gnawed at the feeling she'd begun to have about him.

But his next words didn't help. "What do rights matter?" he asked, his mouth twisted. "I didn't become a success waiting around for rights."

"So you trespassed on my land," she said, and she might have added "on my heart." "And you bought White Acres behind my back, never letting me know what you intended to do with it. And when you saw me last night, you were ready to take me off with you knowing I didn't have any idea who you were."

"Why did you come back?" she'd asked. "To find you," he'd answered. And she'd believed him.

Fire simmered behind her dark eyes. "Do you ever consider anyone else's rights, Michael Donovan? Or do you only think about yourself, about getting what *you* want, when *you* want it?"

He sighed, half turning away. "I'd hoped that a night's sleep would cool you down. But I see you're going to need more time," he said casually, glancing at his watch. "I've got business in San Francisco tonight, but I'll be back in the morning. I'll come by and see if you're ready to listen to reason then."

"No!" she cried, clenching her hands into tight fists. "Don't come back tomorrow. Don't come back at all."

Despite what she said, she knew in her secret heart that he could make things better. If he said just the right thing, or looked at her just the right way, they could begin to build a bridge. She waited, almost holding her breath, but his words dashed her hopes.

"All right, Pamela." He spoke in a soft voice, but his eyes were hard. "If that's what you want. I'll wait for you to come to me."

"Never!"

"You'll come," he said with offhand confidence. He didn't touch her but his gaze was intimate, making her feel as though he knew her as well as she knew herself. She put a hand to her throat as though to ward him off. "The magic still works between us—that magic from the day on the hill. I know you feel it, too. And once you've accepted what's going to happen at White Acres..." He smiled. "We'll go on from where we left off."

His arrogance left her speechless. Suddenly he stepped forward, taking her face in his hands. "It's not going to be so bad, Pamela," he told her earnestly. "I'm leaving the main house the way it was when you lived there. Once you're used to the idea, I want you to come out and look at the plans. I think you might even like them."

Plans. What did she care for plans? Oh, she cared all right, on a certain level. She loved White Acres. It would always be a part of her. But the White Acres she loved was gone forever. It would live on in her heart, and nowhere else. She realized that now. She was still in mourning, but ready to go on. He'd bought the land, and she hoped he treated it well. She didn't think she would ever like the idea of a resort being built there. It offended her sense of place, her feeling for history. But the initial shock was over. What she couldn't forget was something much deeper. Couldn't he see that?

It was the deception that bothered her most. It was his casual assumption that he could do whatever he wanted. If he would only say he was sorry, or let her know in some way that he regretted what he'd done.

He'd made a fool of her, and he didn't seem to understand that she might feel angry and humiliated.

Maybe he wasn't sorry. Maybe he didn't regret a thing. Didn't he know how close she'd come to loving him? Didn't he care?

"I don't want to see your plans," she heard herself saying wildly. "There are plenty of people in this town who don't want a resort here. You just might find your plans being stopped, Mr. Donovan."

In desperation, she was snatching at Jeremy's suggestions, even though she really had no intention of trying to stop the resort. But she had to use the weapons she had at her disposal, and when she saw Michael's jaw tighten and a white line appear around his mouth, she knew she'd hit a nerve.

His hands left her and she staggered slightly, reaching out to support herself on the counter.

"One thing you can count on, Pamela Starbuck," he said almost menacingly, "is the resort being built, and right on schedule. Nothing—nothing—is going to stop it."

He was gone before she could answer and she followed him to the door, turning the sign to read Closed. Then she went upstairs to the apartment she shared with her sister. There on the dresser in her bedroom was the garland of gardenias, wilted now, but still fragrant. She picked it up and held the soft flowers against her cheek, then started toward the wastebasket. She hesitated, dangling the garland over the container, but somehow she couldn't bring herself to actually drop it in. Instead, hardly allowing herself to think about what she was doing, she pulled open a drawer and threw in the wreath, then slammed it shut again and hurried downstairs to turn the sign around.

There was no sense in letting herself get caught in a spiral of depression. It was best to keep busy. To keep busy, and to prepare herself for the next time she would see Michael—for she was sure that time wouldn't be far off.

CHAPTER FIVE

PAMELA THOUGHT very hard that afternoon and all through the night. She knew her mind would be flooded with misery over Michael, if she allowed her thoughts to follow their natural course. Instead, she fended off despair by puzzling out what to do with the shop.

"I think I'm beginning to get an idea," she told Suzy the next morning as they sat over their orange juice and toast. "It's not fully developed yet, but I've got bits and pieces of it."

"Give me a hint," Suzy demanded, popping a square of buttered toast into her mouth and looking as pleased as a well-fed cat.

Pamela frowned. Puppy love was all very well, but perhaps she ought to warn her sister.... She stopped herself in time. What a cynic she was becoming! If she wasn't careful, she'd wind up like one of those people who sees disasters down every road. She didn't want to rain on Suzy's holiday. Jeremy seemed nice enough. Not every man was as ruthless and ready to bend the truth as Michael. She couldn't let him and the things he'd done poison her life.

"A hint," she repeated quietly. "All right." She raised the sun-colored juice to her lips, enjoying the coolness of the glass before she took a sip. "Close your eyes." She smiled the dutiful way her little sister did what she was told. "Let your mind travel back in time." She waited a moment, allowing a dreamy look to soften Suzy's face before she went on. "Think about all the people who have come through this valley over the ages. Think about the Indians, the Miwoks who came through in the spring and the fall, traveling between the snows of Yosemite and the green foothills. Think of the Spaniards and Mexicans who came here chasing the Indians who'd stolen their horses. Think of the early mountain men who came here following grizzlies and other game, and then the Gold Rush, which drew Americans and Mexicans and Chinese and Russians and Peruvians. All those different cultures converging right here in our valley."

She paused dramatically and Suzy opened her eyes, saying blandly, "So?"

"So?" Pamela pretended to glare at her sister. "Don't you see? We tend to forget all that history. We live our modern television-and-jet-travel lives and we forget where we came from, the things that made us what we are."

Suzy looked pained. Her face plainly said that she didn't think her sister was making too much sense. "And you think the shop is somehow going to remind us of all those things?"

Pamela smiled into her orange juice. "Yes."

Suzy sighed. History had never been her favorite subject. Their conversation reminded her of school and studying dull facts, and she didn't see how any of this was going to help the shop. "How?"

"We're going to specialize in handicrafts and artwork from those cultures."

That was just about what her sister had been afraid of. "You mean open a museum?" Suzy asked skeptically.

"No." Enthusiasm was beginning to ignite her mood. Even Suzy's frowns couldn't stifle it. "Well, maybe, kind of. Don't you see? We need something to make us special, something to set us apart from all the other little knickknack gift shops along the highway. We need a draw, something that will make people mention us to their friends. We'll specialize in things from the different historical eras, maybe print brochures to go with each item, giving some background on the culture it comes from. We'll set up the displays as historical interpretations. People won't just be buying gifts, they'll be buying a little piece of history."

Suzy smiled at her sister's excitement. She was being won over, despite herself. "I think maybe I like it after all," she said softly. "But—" she looked down at the crusts of toast still on her plate "—this isn't for the local trade, is it, Pamela? You're going for tourists now."

Pamela rose and carried her plate to the sink. "Of course," she said stoutly. "That's where the money is."

There was a tense silence, then Suzy slowly asked, "Are you doing this to make money—or to compete with Michael Donovan's resort shops?"

Pamela froze, her back to Suzy. Just how much had Suzy noticed? She hadn't said a word, hadn't asked a question, but she'd seen what Pamela had done at Philip's party. She'd seen Pamela in Michael's arms.

The idea of their little shop competing with the large-scale business Michael planned was ludicrous, but she had to admit there was a thread of truth in what Suzy suggested. Well, so what? Sometimes the spirit of competition was just what was needed to start the creative juices flowing. She briskly turned on the water to rinse her dishes and turned it off again before she faced Suzy.

"I'm doing this to make a living for the two of us," she said evenly. "I'll do whatever I have to do to keep us from sinking out here in the big world. And you'd better be prepared to do the same."

Brave words. What did they really mean? She wasn't sure she knew. But she didn't want to think about painful things, so she concentrated on her renovation ideas.

"We'll set things up sequentially," she told Suzy later, as they opened the shop. "When a visitor first enters, he'll see the Indian display. Moving in he'll come to the Mexican artifacts, and so on."

"Ending with the modern high-priced stuff right by the cash register?" Suzy put in pointedly.

Pamela grinned, refusing to be provoked. "Of course. Now if you'll help me, I'm going to pack away all these fur-lined pot holders the old owners left. And these purple latex egg cups...."

They spent the morning winnowing through their inventory. By lunchtime they had cleared quite a bit of space for Pamela's new idea.

"What are we going to do with all this junk?" Suzy wailed, flourishing a cast-off wall hanging of cowrie shells and painted macaroni. "We can't just throw it out."

"Church bazaars," Pamela announced. "Girl Scout carnivals. Indian guide swap meets. We'll donate so much stuff, they'll think we're crazy and come by just to see what's going on here."

"I hope you know what you're doing."

She didn't, though. She didn't even want to. She was driven by a surge of nervous energy that didn't leave her time to stop and make sure of anything.

Suzy left to meet Jeremy for lunch again, and while she was gone Pamela half expected Michael to show up. But no one came in at all. When the young couple returned, she was grateful to have someone to talk to.

Even so, all she really wanted to talk about was her plans. "Has Suzy told you what we're doing here? It's so exciting!"

She could tell there was something else on their minds, but she went on, anyway. "There's a California Indian group in Sacramento that makes baskets and bows and ceremonial costumes, and even little mortars and pestles like the Miwoks used to grind their cornmeal with. I've called them and ordered their catalog."

Jeremy had no interest in setting up museum shops. He stood before her, eyes burning like an old-world prophet's waiting for her to finish. Her voice faltered at the end of her speech, and she watched him uncomfortably.

"We're going to fight it," he said at last, his words booming through the little shop. "We're going to fight it, and we're going to win."

Pamela glanced at Suzy. "What's all this about?" she asked.

Suzy licked her lips and stepped forward. "Well, Jeremy thinks he's got a way to stop Michael Donovan from converting White Acres into a resort. He's contacted some friends in Berkeley."

"The first thing we do is get our side into the local paper," Jeremy said, hitting a fist into his palm.

"Then we hold an information meeting for the citizens. When we've worked up enough support, we force the mayor to call a town meeting."

It was all very well to tell Michael she knew people who might oppose his plans, but allying herself with this kind of rebellion was another matter. She watched Jeremy, bemused. She rather admired his fire, but it wasn't her style. She glanced at Suzy, whose eyes were wide and full of wonder. Jeremy obviously had a convert there. But she'd better make it clear that she couldn't back full-scale war.

"Wait a minute, Jeremy," she finally said. "I'm... impressed with all you know and flattered that you would care so much about White Acres. But I think we have to face facts here. We sold White Acres. Mr. Donovan can do what he wants with it."

Jeremy's hazel eyes snapped. "Unless the people of this town don't let him," he said. "They can stop him if they want to. It's happened before. I've spoken to people who've stopped shopping malls from being built, people who've fought apartment complexes and condominium conversions. All we need is the will." He slapped his thin hand down on the counter. "We can do it here, too."

Jeremy certainly had a fine crusading spirit, but she couldn't help thinking he ought to use it to more productive ends. Somehow her intuition told her that a struggle between him and Michael Donovan was a losing battle from the start. He needed bigger guns than any she could see available.

"What we need," he announced dramatically, pointing to Pamela, "is you."

"Me?" she squeaked.

"Yes, you. I heard you the other night when you spoke to the crowd. They respect you. They really listened to what you had to say. And a lot of them care about you and the Starbuck family. You'd be surprised. I've talked to people in town and I find a lot of them feel really bad about what happened to you. They think you deserved better. You could sway votes."

"Sway votes?" She wasn't even tempted. It had been one thing to stand before the crowd and say what she thought that other night, with anger to fuel her rhetoric. It was another to plan a speaking campaign. That would pit her against Michael. He made her angry, but he also made her tremble. She didn't think a public forum was where she wanted to test just which of those emotions was the stronger.

"I can't, Jeremy," she told him. "And I really can't promise to back you in any substantial way, because I don't think there's much point in it. Michael is 'progress' and those wheels will grind you down."

"You won't fight for your own land?"

She sighed. "It's not my land any longer. It's too late to fight. Anything you do now will only create hard feelings in the town and divide people." She shook her head. "No, do what you feel you must, but leave me out of it."

Still, she thought about Jeremy and his campaign as she walked across the street to the little bank where they did their business. What if she and Jeremy *could* sway public opinion and get a vote against Miracle Development? She had a brief and delicious picture of herself walking into Michael's office, waving a petition and ordering him to stop the bulldozers. Delicious, but hardly likely.

She went into the bank, filled out her deposit slip for the three very small checks they'd received that day and stood in line for a teller, nodding at Mr. Grayson, the grocer, smiling at Irma Sobel, principal of the local elementary school, and then stopped to listen.

Michael was in the bank. She could hear his deep voice. Once she'd recognized it, the sound seemed to wrap her in warmth, tantalizing her with his nearness, and she had to square her shoulders and bite her lip to keep from looking in his direction.

She knew she'd have to get used to this. Whatley was a small town and if they both were going to live here, they were destined to meet often. She only hoped it wouldn't always make her heart beat so fast, and her knees feel so weak.

He was coming closer. He seemed to be discussing something with the president of the bank, who was now showing him to the door. She stood very still in line, not seeing anything, only hearing his voice, not distinguishing words. Then the voice stopped, paused, and she held her breath.

She knew he saw her. She could feel his crystal-blue gaze sweeping over her. She needed all her strength to stay where she was and not turn. Could he see the excruciating redness creeping up her neck? Probably. But she wouldn't turn.

When she heard him speak again, he was almost at the door. He wasn't going to talk to her. He'd accepted her decision, after all. She heard his voice once more, saying goodbye, and then he was gone. The blood seemed to drain from her body and she had to put out a hand to regain her balance, to keep from falling.

"Next, please." The teller had to call three times before she heard, and when she got to the window, it took a moment to remember why she was there. Nevertheless, she was proud of herself. She hadn't given in to the overwhelming temptation to look at him. She'd held her ground. Maybe there was some hope of forgetting him.

That hope seemed fainter as the days went by. She didn't actually see him again, but he was everywhere she went. As she and Suzy culled the strange assortment of objects that had come with the shop and traveled all over the valley trying to find sources for the new lines they wanted, he was always in her mind. Michael Donovan was in the background of every decision she made. Was she going to spend the rest of her life reacting to him?

But they did accomplish some progress in setting up the sort of shop they wanted. A few telephone calls to San Francisco put Pamela in touch with a South American importer who promised to deliver Peruvian rugs and weavings for her perusal, and a local restaurateur had a cousin in Chinatown who stocked just about any Chinese object she could imagine.

And then Suzy made a Russian purchase. She did it while Pamela was visiting a craft fair in Merced. She claimed an old Russian woman had driven up in a van and shown her the items, and she'd bought them on the spot.

"I knew you were going to love them, too," Suzy crowed as Pamela walked into the shop that afternoon.

Pamela tried to smile, then stared again at the row of six fat, knee-high ceramic ducks waddling in order of descending size from the front door out into the street. They were yellow with big, flat orange feet, and superior smirks—and each duck wore a colorful babushka. Russian grandmother ducks. Impossible creatures.

"Aren't they adorable?" Suzy crooned. "I thought they would look best there, where people driving by could see them. They'll bring in customers—I just know it."

Well, what could she say? After all, Suzy had as much right to a voice in the decisions as Pamela did. And yet...and yet...what about their plan? Russian grandmother ducks didn't quite fit into the scheme of things. Even though Russians had explored Northern California, and Russian men had joined the Gold Rush, Pamela had never heard of them bringing their grandmothers along.

"They're certainly adorable," she agreed carefully, then tilted her head to the side and went on hesitantly, trying to be tactful. "But we can't leave them there. They're totally out of place at the front door. They don't go with the Indian display at all." She could see resistance growing in Suzy's eyes and she got a little wild herself. "You can't have a sequential history of the valley and start out with a welcome from Russian ducks with bandanas on their heads. It isn't logical," she added helplessly.

When Suzy took a stand, she could be stubborn as a desert tortoise. "Logical!" she cried, her lower lip trembling. "Since when did you become so darn logical? I wasn't thinking of logic. I was thinking of...of fun."

Pamela felt a sense of desperation. Wasn't Suzy ever going to grow up? This was serious business. This was their livelihood. "Fun?" she scoffed, on the attack now. "What do Russian ducks have to do with fun? Russian ducks have to do with melancholy and sorrow and the suffering of life. That's all they know, the agony of the Russian soul." She stopped, blinking rapidly, realizing she'd become carried away.

Suzy eyed her warily and Pamela regretted her own lack of restraint. It wasn't just Suzy or the ducks. It was everything. The whole world seemed to rest on her shoulders. And the man of her dreams had turned out to be a nightmare. But that wasn't Suzy's fault. It was time for a truce.

Suzy was obviously thinking the same thing. She glanced at the ducks, then back at her sister. "I didn't know it was all sadness," she murmured, still a bit defensive.

Pamela sighed, giving her a half smile. "Yes, it really is," she said softly. "It's ingrained in Russian culture. Everything's sad."

Suzy's lower lip thrust out stubbornly. "What about balalaikas?" she retorted.

"Balalaikas?" Pamela echoed blankly.

"You know. Those guitarlike things Russians play that wild, *happy* music on." There was triumph in her eyes now.

Pamela looked at the triumph and at that lower lip and felt a wave of affection for her baby sister. It was time to end this silly argument. "Balalaikas!" She nodded and snapped her fingers. "What a good idea! We should have at least one in our display, and a few more in stock just in case." She smiled tentatively at her sister. "Where do you suppose we'll have to go for balalaikas?"

Suzy met her gaze for a long moment, then finally returned the smile. "I don't know." She grinned, ready to be friends again. "Let's try San Francisco. They're bound to have someone who makes them there. They've got everything else weird in the world."

They both laughed and, in a shared impulse, moved toward each other for a lingering hug. "Leave your ducks where they are," Pamela said. "At least for now. We'll see how they survive the foot traffic and being taken in every night."

For the time being, the ducks had found a home in the middle of pre-Spanish California.

Things were shaping up and Pamela was pleased with the progress they were making. Friends who stopped by didn't quite understand her urgency, but in the main they were complimentary. Jeremy kept a watchful eye on the changes, but he was more concerned with campaign strategy than with hinging llama-wool rugs. Philip offered to lend them the samplers his great-grandmother had embroidered in 1859, as she'd journeyed across the desert in a covered wagon. And Bernice loved the ducks.

"Have you seen Michael Donovan lately?" Suzy asked one afternoon, her voice just a shade too casual.

Pamela looked up sharply. "Why on earth would you ask a question like that?" she demanded.

Suzy tried unsuccessfully to hold back a grin. "I saw you two in the garden at Philip's the other night. I know you're at odds over the development, but you seemed so...friendly."

Pamela turned away. "That was before I knew who he was and what he was planning." She slammed an accounts book shut and tossed it onto a shelf. "He's the enemy now. Remember? I would think that you, of all people, with Jeremy trumpeting this campaign business..."

Suzy brushed that off. "It's Jeremy's crusade, not mine. He's into principles. I believe in relationships."

Pamela swung around to glare at her. "Forget it."

"But don't you see? If you and Michael Donovan were close, maybe you could influence what he does with White Acres..."

Pamela left the room without waiting to hear the rest, and Suzy didn't dare bring the subject up again.

A week later Bernice invited her for dinner. "You need a break from all this work," she said.

Pamela hesitated. She wasn't ready to face a horde of people all interested in the shop and asking questions about it. She wanted to wait until everything was finished and she could be proud and sure in her answers. "I don't think I'm ready for a party," she began, but Bernice waved her into silence.

"Not a party, just a cozy dinner with your closest friends." She grinned. "Namely, me and Fred. And I can't exclude Jeremy, as he's still staying with me. Oh, and bring Suzy."

Pamela couldn't very well refuse. But a thought struck her. "You're not going to make me ask Philip, are you?"

Bernice was quick to reassure her. Too quick, really. "Not at all, not at all. Just bring your own sweet self. And Suzy, of course. Why not let Jeremy pick you up at six? Then you won't have to bother with the car."

All of which should have warned her, but didn't. She spent the late afternoon blithely preparing for the dinner, without one suspicious thought, despite all the clues Bernice had given.

She brushed her hair until the copper highlights shone, then slipped into a simple wool dress of forest green that clung flatteringly to her slender form. "No punk costume tonight?'' she called to Suzy who was in the bathroom putting the finishing touches on her makeup. She emerged in a baby-blue dress with a white Peter Pan collar, her blond hair curling softly around her face.

"Oh, honestly," she said, expressing scorn for her foibles of old. "I've grown up, Pamela. I don't need that sort of thing any longer."

Pamela laughed and reached into the closet for her coat. "Older men will do that to you," she murmured.

"Do what?"

"Turn you old overnight," she teased. Suzy gave her a blank stare that said she hadn't the slightest idea what her sister was talking about, and they both left their little apartment as Jeremy drove up.

The ride out to Bernice's took about ten minutes. She still lived in the lovely old house she'd grown up in. The land had been sold long ago, but the house remained, with a few beautifully landscaped acres around it. Bernice had a comfortable life with the money from the sale of the land. She'd married young and regretted it quickly, but now she was divorced and about to remarry. Fred was a local dairyman, short on conversation but long on goodwill, and he seemed to love Bernice very much. Pamela was looking forward to a relaxing evening with the two of them.

Her expectations fell apart as soon as Jeremy pulled into the long circular drive toward the low, ranch-style house. She saw the blood-red Ferrari immediately, and though she'd never seen Michael's car, she knew there was no one else in the valley who would own a car like that. Her fingers tightened on the clutch purse she was carrying, and her first impulse was to order Jeremy to turn around and drive her home.

She thought better of it immediately. Running away would only prove she was frightened. She had to brazen this out, just as she'd done at the bank the other day.

"Whose car?" she asked Jeremy as they parked near the entrance. She still clung to a shred of hope.

"I don't know," he answered. "Somebody rich." And his young face hardened, ready to do battle with all the unworthy rich people of the world.

But Suzy knew. Pamela could see it in her eyes. She and Bernice had obviously devised this whole thing between them. Pamela was enraged, but she could do nothing about it now. Nothing direct, at any rate.

Tossing her head, she walked quickly from the car and arrived at the front door just as Bernice opened it. Pamela gave her an exaggerated smile. "Hello, darling," she said, emphasizing the endearment in a way she usually did not, so her friend would get the picture. "It seems you already have company."

Bernice had the grace to look a bit uncomfortable. "Oh, it's just, ah, Michael Donovan. I happened to run into him the other day..." Her voice trailed off and Pamela smiled brightly.

"Michael who?" she asked loudly. "I didn't catch the last name."

Bernice looked nervous. "M—Michael Donovan. The...the man who..."

"Oh, not that devastatingly handsome man who bought White Acres? Bernice, what a coup!" She was angry and she wanted her sarcasm to kindle Bernice's guilt and burn Michael's ears, as well. But to her dismay the ploy backfired. She looked past Bernice and saw Michael standing there, drink in hand, amusement lurking in his blue eyes, and the moment she met

his gaze she knew he thought this little charade was
being played out for his benefit. He thought she'd put
Bernice up to it! He thought she was scheming to re-
sume their relationship without humbly coming to him
first as he'd claimed she would. Fury choked her, and
she was breathless.

CHAPTER SIX

"HELLO, PAMELA," he said, moving forward to greet her. "It's nice to see you again."

He was approaching her as though intending to kiss her cheek, and she quickly stuck out her hand to forestall any such ideas. He shook it solemnly, though a smile tugged at the corners of his mouth.

She glared up at him, hardening her heart against the natural warmth of his gaze. "Hello," she said quickly, jerking back her hand. "What a surprise to find you here."

His grin infuriated her. "Is it?" he asked skeptically. "I hope it's a pleasant one."

She avoided answering, as dearly as she would have loved telling him the truth. But she couldn't do that. She couldn't stand there, with her hands on her hips, shrieking that she hadn't known he was going to be at Bernice's, that she wouldn't have come if she had known, that she had no interest in seeing him again, now or ever. Well, almost no interest. Because she had to admit that she felt something very special for this provoking man.

Confused and upset, barely noticing that Bernice was encouraging Jeremy to take Suzy to see the horses, she walked quickly toward the living room, smiling at Fred and inclining her cheek for his kiss.

"What'll you have?" he asked, his large, bearlike body looking warm and comforting in a shaggy Shetland sweater, his brown eyes beaming at his favorite of all Bernice's friends.

A good stiff belt of poison, she thought, but managed to smile and say aloud, "White wine would be lovely."

Holding her drink, she walked to the sliding glass door that overlooked the rolling lawns and the forest, now painted the reds and yellows of fall. It was getting dark, but she could see Jeremy and Suzy heading toward the stables. Behind her, she could hear Bernice chattering nervously. Pamela knew she would have to turn and face them all soon. But for just a moment she looked out over the land and tried to draw some strength from it.

"Michael was just telling us about himself when you came, Pam," Bernice said, her voice making it clear she expected Pamela to join the conversation.

"Was he?" She turned slowly and faced Michael. "How fascinating."

His blue eyes narrowed slightly. He was a bit puzzled by her animosity. Good. Let him be puzzled. Let him be anything but so infuriatingly assured that he knew exactly what she wanted.

"Oh, it is fascinating," Bernice gushed in a very irritating manner. She knew there was an off-note here and she wasn't sure how to deal with it, so her usual social aplomb was slipping. Ordinarily Pamela would have been quick to rescue her. But this time she had other things on her mind. "He grew up so poor, in a tenement in Seattle, and here he is so..." She was about to say "so rich," but realizing just how tacky that would sound she stopped, eyes wide and searching, hand to throat.

"Yes, isn't he?" Pamela supplied helpfully. "And aren't we lucky?" She sat on the edge of a chair that faced the couch where Michael reclined beside Bernice. "Tell us, Mr. Donovan, how you made that long and difficult climb from a Seattle tenement to our little valley."

His blue eyes sparkled. He'd decided he liked her barbs. "It wasn't easy," he said, leaning back into the soft pillows of the couch as though he were perfectly at home. "There were some very lean years."

She nodded in mock sympathy. "And a lot of people to step on. I suppose."

Bernice gasped. "Pamela!" she hissed in horror.

But Michael laughed. "Sorry," he told her comfortably. "I'm afraid it didn't work quite that way. You see, when I was twelve, my mother married Marshall Bentworth. And from then on, it was only a matter of proving myself to him."

Pamela waved a hand. "Which was, of course, a piece of cake, you being so wonderfully talented."

His grin was wide. "Of course."

It was clear she wasn't going to shake his confidence no matter what she did or said. The only thing she accomplished by trying was to make herself look like a waspish fool. She could see only one other path, and she took it. Sitting back in her chair, slowly sipping her wine, she completely opted out of the conversation.

She was determined not to let Michael think he'd intimidated her, though, and she met his gaze firmly, giving him a glare, a supercilious smile, a questioning look, all in turn, depending on what he and Bernice

were saying. Little by little, he was becoming en-
trapped by her glances, answering with his own
amused stare, until the electricity between them
seemed to snap and flare. Bernice found herself alone,
chattering on and on, until she too lapsed into silence, gazing helplessly from Michael to Pamela, and
finally looking to Fred for help. Fred smiled and
puffed on his pipe.

When the maid announced dinner, Bernice's sigh of
relief was audible.

"May I?" Michael surprised Pamela by offering his
arm. She rose and accepted, slipping her hand into the
crook of his elbow, starting a small and mostly unde-
tectable tug-of-war as he tried to press her hand
against him, while she resisted fiercely, pulling back,
a stiff smile on her face.

As they entered the formal dining room with its
polished wood and sparkling chandelier, Jeremy and
Suzy burst into the room, laughing as though they'd
had a marvelous time, and Michael was forced to let
go of Pamela so he could be introduced. Pamela took
the opportunity to move toward the seat farthest from
where Michael stood, hoping that Bernice's schemes
hadn't included seating arrangements. As she brushed
by Suzy she whispered, through clenched teeth, "You
and Bernice are going to pay for this." She'd barely
settled herself when she found Michael sliding into the
chair beside her.

She glanced at him sideways, then looked straight
ahead, hands in her lap. "I didn't plan this, you
know," she murmured, her voice covered by the confusion of the others finding their seats.

"Didn't you? And here I thought you'd set it up to
torture me."

He'd leaned toward her to speak and the warmth of his breath tickled her cheek. She felt something twist inside and had to close her eyes for just a moment to hold back an involuntary shudder. She'd never been affected by a man this way. His voice sent a thrill through her bloodstream, his touch melted her resolve, his humor undercut her defenses. It would be so easy to love him, and it was so hard to keep herself from showing it.

She was quiet during dinner. Bernice always served a lavish meal and tonight's was no exception. The first course was shrimp toasts cut into flower shapes and browned to a delicate hue. Duck in orange sauce, scallion pancakes and Chinese broccoli were presented for the main course, and beautiful Napoleon with raspberry sauce completed the feast. But Pamela could hardly force down a bite.

Bernice and Jeremy provided most of the conversation, with Michael adding a word here and there. Suzy looked sad and uncomfortable, occasionally sending Pamela a worried look. She realized their matchmaking hadn't worked the way they'd planned, and she was obviously sorry she'd had anything to do with it.

Thinking about the evening later, Pamela was surprised that Jeremy kept his self-control as long as he did. It didn't occur to her at the time that he might get on his soapbox. Her mind was too full of the man beside her to give Jeremy a thought. But once the younger man was launched into the sermon about his current obsession, she realized that a confrontation had been inevitable from the start.

Bernice began the process when she asked how the work at White Acres was coming along. Until that moment, everyone had carefully avoided the topic, so it caught attention all around the table. Jeremy's jaw was clenched as he restrained himself from jumping into the fray.

"We're on schedule," Michael answered blandly. "We're hoping to be open for business by Easter week."

It was at this point that Jeremy began to simmer, but no one noticed as Bernice quickly trilled, "Oh, how wonderful! I've seen the plans, and yesterday I went by and your foreman showed me around. Pamela, you have to go out and see the place. They're leaving the house just as it always was. You'll feel better about the whole thing, I'm sure, if you just go out and take a look..."

Better? Better than what? She looked around the table and wondered what they were thinking. Had any of them known what it was like to have their ancestral home torn from them by forces they couldn't control? Had any of them carried the burden of guilt left by generations of pioneers whose legacy was being sullied by commercial interests? And Bernice told her she would feel better about the whole thing if only she accepted it.

She took a sip of wine to calm herself. She knew she was bordering on the irrational. White Acres was sold. Michael was in charge. There was nothing left to say and it was time she came to terms with that. She'd told Jeremy she wouldn't join his fight. And yet every instinct made her want to rail at Michael and tell him exactly what she thought of him. She couldn't do that, not here. But she would do what she could.

"I'm sure Mr. Donovan is doing a marvelous job," she said slowly and with great dignity. "He's told us himself how talented he is. White Acres should be a showcase when he gets through with it.''

Everyone stared at her for a brief moment, then began to talk at once. Michael was chuckling and he leaned close and whispered, ''You're not going to give up without a real rousing fight, are you?''

''Not on your life,'' she snapped back, without really knowing what they were both referring to.

''Hey, Donovan!'' Jeremy's voice won out over the others, and everyone turned to look at him. ''What gives you the right to come into a community and change it to suit your purposes?''

Michael smiled but Pamela could see the hardening in his eyes. ''What kind of right do you think I need, Jeremy?''

''The consent of the people,'' he returned immediately. ''The will of the electorate.''

Michael raised a quizzical eyebrow. ''Do you know something about this hypothetical element I've been missing?'' he asked quietly.

Jeremy banged the table with his fist. ''Yes, I do. This is a peaceful rural town and the people want it to stay that way. You haven't leveled with them, Donovan. You haven't told them about the pollution and the traffic and the crime your little resort will bring upon them.''

Michael's eyes looked black. ''Why should I bother to tell them,'' he answered softly, ''when you're so ready to do it for me?''

''I am ready.'' Jeremy jumped up. ''The town is going to turn against you, Donovan. Pamela and I are going to see to it.''

Pamela stirred in protest, but the conversation slipped right by her.

"You can do what you like," Michael said with steely calm. "Talk all you want. But if you try to interfere in any way with the work going on at White Acres, you'll have me to deal with." He turned to look at Pamela. "Both of you."

Pamela had no intention of doing anything of the kind, but she wasn't about to tell him that. She lifted her chin and held his gaze without saying a word, vaguely aware of Bernice fluttering about the table like a frightened hen.

"Jeremy," Bernice was scolding. "I'll thank you to sit down and mind your manners! You don't speak to a guest in my house that way!"

Jeremy backed away from her, but his glance was scornful. "Then I'd better go, because I can't stay here and keep from saying what I feel." He motioned to Suzy. "Come on, let's get out of here." And he disappeared from the room.

"Bernice..." Suzy looked from one face to another, obviously torn.

"Oh, go on," Bernice sighed. "See if you can calm him down."

Suzy kissed her cheek, glanced pitifully at her sister and flew after Jeremy. Pamela rose. "Perhaps I'd better go, too," she began, but Michael's hand was around her wrist in a second.

"Sit down," he said quietly. "We're not finished."

And for some strange reason, she did as he ordered, sinking into the chair like a rag doll with no will of its own. She could hear Jeremy's car speeding down the driveway—the car she was supposed to be riding home in—while Bernice apologized over and over again.

"I knew he'd been saying a lot of silly things lately, but I didn't pay any attention. I had no idea he would be so rude! I'm so sorry, Michael."

"No problem." Michael's smile had returned. "He's got a right to his opinion."

"He's always been a willful kid, but then how could he help it? His father, my cousin Gerald, used to take him along to sit-ins and strikes and peace rallies when he was a little boy in the sixties. He grew up living in hippie communes and learning protest as a way of life."

"He seems normal enough, doesn't he?" said Fred in one of his rare comments. "Nice kid when he's not all het up."

"What happened to his mother?" Pamela asked, grateful for a topic other than White Acres.

"Oh, she left for India years ago. Went to study the sitar or something like that. We never heard from her again."

Pamela glanced at Michael, then away. "And how about Gerald? Whatever happened to him?"

Bernice laughed. "You won't believe it. They lived like Gypsies all those years, then when Jeremy was ready to go to college, Gerald realized they'd better get some money together, so he cut his hair, got himself a real-estate license, and now he's in the millionaire's club in Fresno."

"Incredible," Pamela agreed at bit vacantly. She had a hard time keeping her mind on Bernice's story. Her thoughts were full of the man who sat beside her. Twisting her fingers around her wrist she could still feel the imprint of his hand. Why should that excite her? Was she going crazy?

The rest of the evening passed in a misty dream. They lingered over coffee and told stories and laughed, but Pamela heard hardly a word. She didn't turn to look at Michael but she could feel him, feel his will, feel his hard, lean body. In some mysterious way, he was in control of her now. She didn't know how it had happened, but she didn't seem to have the energy to fight it.

When he announced that he was driving her home she merely nodded, then turned to thank Bernice and Fred. After all, this was only to be expected. Fred lived farther out in the country and there was certainly no sign that Jeremy would be back soon. Bernice couldn't have planned it better if she'd tried. She threw her hostess a suspicious glance. Could she really have planned this, right down to the final detail? No, even Bernice couldn't have foreseen how Jeremy would act. Pecking her friend on the cheek, Pamela whispered, "Matchmaking is a lost art, Bernice, and I don't think you should try to find it." She treasured Bernice's little gasp and look of distress all the way to Michael's car.

The Ferrari was a powerful car, and she found herself clutching the seat with her fingernails as they roared down the driveway. But Michael was a sure and skillful driver, and she began to relax quickly enough. The car raced along the highway, its headlights cutting a swath through the rural darkness, the only sign of life for miles. They seemed cut off from the rest of the world, suspended in time. Neither said a word to the other, but they didn't need to.

The lights of Whatley broke the spell. Pamela sat up a little straighter as they came into town. Michael seemed to stiffen, too. He pulled up in front of the store and turned off the engine.

"You're awfully quiet," he said, making no move to get out and come around to her door.

"I don't have anything to say," she replied, not looking at him.

"You don't have anything at all to say to me?" he asked.

She stirred uncomfortably. "What do you think I should say?"

"Well, you could start with an apology."

Outraged, she swung around to look at him, but his eyes were sparkling in the dark. Did he think she should make excuses for Jeremy? Or offer an explanation of what Jeremy had said? Or ask forgiveness for conspiring to set him up for the evening? He could think again. "An apology!" she sputtered. "For what?"

He lifted a lock of her hair, twisting it slowly around his finger, staring at it rather than into her eyes. "For destroying my peace of mind," he said softly. "For making me waste my time daydreaming about you. For getting between me and what I have to do."

She sat very still, hardly breathing. A part of her wanted to laugh and reach out to take him in her arms and hold him close and tell him she was sorry, but that was the part of her he had crushed by his deception. He'd touched her in a way no man had before. That was something she couldn't forget. And then he'd hurt her badly. That was something she mustn't forget. Much as she wanted to, she couldn't trust him.

"I have a feeling nothing really gets between you and what you have to do," she said instead. "Now, if you don't mind, I want to go in." She reached for the door handle but he tugged on the lock of hair, forcing her to stay where she was.

"What's the matter, Pamela?" he asked evenly. "Why are you letting this happen?"

She glanced into his shining gaze, then away again. "I don't know what you're talking about."

"Yes, you do. You respond to me. When I touch you, or speak to you, I can see you tremble like...like a violin begging to be played." His hand went to her cheek, and she had to stifle a tiny moan of pleasure. "But when I make a move toward you, you draw back. You erect barriers to keep me away." His warm hand cupped her chin. "You've built a brick wall, and every time I take a brick down, you put two more in its place."

She took a deep breath. Was it true? Was he really trying and was she really parrying every attempt to get closer? Perhaps. But he hadn't tried very hard as far as she could see. He would have to do something, say something more explicit before she could begin to trust him again. "Maybe you should stop taking them down," she suggested shakily.

He stared at her for a long moment, then dropped his hand and turned to face the front, shifting away from her. "No, Pamela," he said, his voice hard. "I'm not giving up that easily. I've decided that I want you."

Fear leaped into her throat. "Want me? Want me for what?" She'd never had a man say such a thing to her. He was calmly stating his intentions. He hadn't asked for her permission, or even how she felt about it. Did he think the whole world was there for his pleasure? "As a trophy, to prove another one of your victories?"

He turned to look at her again. His eyes glittered in the shadows but whether with anger or amusement she couldn't tell. "You should know better than that," he said softly.

"I—I'm not sure that I do know better than that."

"Then I'll have to prove it to you, won't I?"

She felt as though she were being smothered. She fumbled for the door handle again and finally found it. Her fingers curled around the cold metal, testing it. It didn't give at all. "How are you going to do that?" she asked.

"I don't know yet. But I'll find a way." He bent toward her and she jerked back, holding her breath, but he was only leaning across to open the door for her. "I'll find a way," he repeated as she stepped out of the car. She looked down at him for a moment, then whirled around and ran to the stairway that led to her rooms above the store.

CHAPTER SEVEN

HE'D SAID HE WANTED HER. No man had ever stated it quite so baldly to her before. Philip would have been shocked.

She stayed awake late that night mulling it over. The man who was destroying her home wanted her. As an extension of his act of possession? To prove he could always get what he wanted? To keep her from becoming active in the protest against his construction? Perhaps it was a combination of all those things. Her head was spinning with the possibilities.

She'd begun the evening sure he was the enemy, and he'd done nothing to change her mind on that score. But he'd proved to her—so easily—just how vulnerable she was to his pursuit. She trembled at his touch, her body aching for more, her heart... No. She wasn't going to admit just how much her heart was involved, even to herself.

He'd said he wanted her, that he was going to prove it and that's exactly what he began to do the very next morning. Pamela had gone to the hardware store down the street to buy the makings for a set of hanging shelves. Mr. Jarner had packed the materials for her and offered to have them delivered.

"That boy of mine ought to be back in about an hour. I'll have him lug everything over then."

But Pamela was anxious to get started. Once she had an idea, she hated to let anything slow her down until she'd put it into action.

"I can handle it," she said confidently, then had second thoughts as she lifted up the long package and tried to balance it and edge out the door at the same time. She felt like a mouse trying to carry a child's teeter-totter across the yard. But one look at Mr. Jarner's skeptical grin was enough to harden her determination.

"You'll never make it—a little girl like you," he said.

Her eyes narrowed and her chin rose and she insisted, "Of course I can do it," and then had to ask him to hold the door. But she did make it out to the sidewalk and she threw back a triumphant smile—and almost ran right into Michael.

He was dressed casually in jeans and a light, short-sleeved shirt, as it was a warm, sunny day. His bare arms looked marvelously strong and muscular, perfect for carrying heavy, awkward parcels. That was what he seemed to think, too.

"Here," he said, reaching out, "let me get that for you."

"No!" she warned, backing away and almost toppling over in the process. "I can do it."

His grin wasn't skeptical, just amused. "I have no doubt you could leap tall buildings in a single bound if you set your mind to it," he said dryly, "but why bother if there's a ladder nearby?" He tapped the edge of her long burden. "Let me take one end while you take the other."

Grudgingly she agreed to let him help. Together they carried it the two blocks to the shop and he maneuvered it in the door. Then, to her surprise, he left.

"See you later," he said, and she had a feeling he meant it. He'd said he'd find a way to prove how he felt about her. But since she wasn't at all sure how that was, she didn't know what to expect. It seemed, though, that he did have a plan. In fact, everyone seemed to have a plan for her future—except her.

Suzy had been full of regrets over the incident at Bernice's. "I'm so sorry we did that to you," she said, admitting that she and Bernice had planned the whole thing from the beginning. "We should never have done it. I know I'd hate it if someone threw me at a guy that way. I promise never ever to do it again!"

Bernice wasn't quite as contrite. "It was for your own good, Pamela," she insisted. "I know I was upset about your selling White Acres, and by rights I should have disliked the new owner...but I don't. And anyone can see that he's crazy about you. Fred and I were invited to the Halstons' the other night and he was there. When all he wanted to talk about was you, I knew right away, and I thought once you two got together... But you're so stubborn that I knew you wouldn't come if I told you I'd invited him. So I went ahead and tricked you." She was actually proud of herself. "After all, he owns White Acres. If you marry him—"

"Bernice! I'm not marrying Michael Donovan. I didn't marry Philip to keep White Acres and I certainly don't intend to marry someone else to do it."

Bernice smiled in a particularly superior and infuriating way. "We'll see," she said slyly.

Pamela vowed to be very careful of any invitations or suggestions that came from Bernice.

True to his word, Michael began to be a regular visitor to the shop. He never stayed, just looked in and said hello whenever he had business in town. He always had a smile for Suzy and a knowing grin for Pamela, and neither of them could resist him for long.

"He's so cute," Suzy said after one of his visits. "You ought to go out with him."

Pamela grimaced. "I don't want to go out with him," she said evenly.

Suzy gave her a teasing glance. "Then maybe I will," she said airily. "I mean, the man obviously needs a woman and..."

"And Jeremy would wring your neck," Pamela retorted, though she couldn't deny her own pang of jealousy at the thought of anyone else going out with Michael, which was the response Suzy had hoped for.

Was she crazy? Could she resent a man so much, and yet still want him? It seemed the two things were not all that incompatible. The more often he came around, the more she wished he would stay.

"Why don't you come for dinner tonight?" Suzy burst out impulsively one day. Jeremy was out of town, and Pamela and Suzy had been planning a quiet evening alone.

Pamela felt a flicker of dread at her sister's words, but there was no way to take back the invitation. Michael agreed to it quickly.

"I'm sorry," Suzy said later. "I just couldn't help myself. Something about his smile..."

Yes, something about his smile. Pamela knew all about that. "Just don't leave me alone with him," she warned her sister.

Suzy fixed soft tacos with a crisp green salad and caramelized flan for dessert. He came into their small apartment, filling the room with his masculine presence, and at first they were all stiff and awkward. But not for long. Soon the three of them were sitting around the small unsturdy table, eating and talking and laughing softly.

Michael, Pamela thought as she watched him, *could charm the evil stepmother into taking Snow White back to her bosom.* She smiled at one of his silly jokes and thought, *And he can charm me, too. How much of all that charm is genuine? How much is just currency to buy what he wants?*

He made them laugh with tales about his ill-fated attempt to play college football and made them damp eyed with stories about how hard his mother had worked after his father disappeared, and left them wide-eyed with descriptions of things he'd seen during a project in a South American jungle.

He can wind us up like little dolls, Pamela thought sadly as they wished him good-night at the door, *and then turn us off again.*

HE ASKED PAMELA to go to dinner with him in Fresno and she accepted, then regretted it, tried to phone him to call it off, but couldn't reach him, so she dressed in her most glamorous gown and waited for him. When she opened the door to his knock her heart leaped at the sight of him and she knew he had only to call and she would come, no matter what she tried to tell herself when she was alone.

Still she had to keep her guard up. She let him in, but stopped him from putting her coat around her shoulders so she could search his gaze. "What exactly are you planning?" she asked softly.

He looked surprised. "Planning?" he repeated. "Do I have to have an ulterior motive to want to see you?"

She hesitated, then reached for her evening bag and played with the golden clasp. "The last time we were alone together you talked as though you were preparing a major assault on my defenses," she reminded him.

"Ah, yes." He grinned, head to the side. "I remember that conversation. Scared you, did I?"

"Of course not," she retorted. "But I just don't want—"

"I tell you what. I'll make you a promise. No direct attack tonight. We'll have a ceasefire." He reached out his hand, inviting her to take it. "Tonight will be exempt from the general warfare." She placed her hand in his and his eyes shone. "Is it a deal?"

She nodded. "It's a deal," she said, something wild and wonderful bubbling up inside her.

It was a long drive down out of the foothills to the flatlands of the San Joaquin Valley. Neither of them talked much, but the silence between them was warm and companionable. The car radio played songs from the fifties and when Michael sang along, his voice was rich and right in tune and he seemed to know every lyric of every song. She found herself laughing and watching him, thinking how very much she liked him.

They ate in an elegant restaurant with food as special for the beautiful way it was served as for the exquisite taste. Because it was in a hotel owned by Miracle Development, they were treated royally. A small jazz combo was playing, and Pamela wished suddenly, irrationally, that it had been a dance band instead. She wanted to be in his arms. She wanted to feel his strength against her, his protection around her. He hadn't touched her since Philip's party, and she was aching for his embrace.

Guilt washed over her as she realized how strong the feeling was. This was the man who was turning a beautiful estate—her beautiful estate—into a tourist trap. Why was she here? How could she enjoy his company like this? She should be fighting him, telling him off. She should be cold as ice, sharp as a razor. Instead she melted at his glance.

Something sizzled and snapped whenever their eyes met. She felt it at the oddest moments, in the shop when Suzy was talking and Pamela looked up and found Michael watching her from the doorway, or when she was crossing the street and Michael drove by and called out a greeting, or when she dropped her accounts book and Michael leaned down to get it for her, his shoulder grazing her nylon-clad knee. There was no denying it. She might not trust him, but she was definitely caught in his spell.

They drove back slowly, enjoying the flat, moonlight-drenched fields of golden grain outside Fresno before they began the climb up into the mountains again. When Michael finally pulled into the parking area beside the shop, they both sat in the car, unwilling to let the evening end. She told him about the time her father had taken her to Mexico for the bullfights and that she'd run away in horror and her father had been forced to get the police to help find her. He told her about the time the police had come looking for him when he was five years old.

"Only I wasn't lost," he said with a grin. "I was a suspect in a kidnapping case."

"What?" She laughed, sure there was a joke in this somewhere.

"No, really. And I did it, too. I took Mary Beth Carver's teddy bear when she wasn't looking and I hid him under my bed."

He was serious. "What turned you to this life of crime?" she asked, eyes sparkling.

"Why did I take the bear?" He frowned slightly, as though he hadn't thought about the motivation behind the act for a long, long time. "Because Mary Beth carried him with her everywhere she went, and Mary Beth always looked so happy," he said softly. "I wasn't really sure why that was, but I thought it might have something to do with her teddy bear. And I wanted to be happy like that, too." He paused, then grinned, wiping away the introspection. "She called him Honey but I named him Gronk."

Pamela had a vivid picture of the little boy whose father had left, the child who tried to find security again with a stolen teddy bear. She wanted to reach for Michael, reach back for that little boy, but she knew such an action wasn't in the rules they were playing by. "Did you give him back?" she asked instead.

He laughed softly. "Of course. Sergeant Kelly lived in our building and acted as a sort of private police force for us all. He came calling and told me a story about good and bad and taking things that belong to other people, and I knew he'd come because of Gronk. I brought him out and got ready for the handcuffs, but Sergeant Kelly let me off with a stern lecture. I didn't have to do any time."

She laughed with him, even though the laughter was touched with a sense of melancholy, and then his manner changed. "You see that moon out there?" he asked softly.

She looked at the full moon riding high like a huge jolly lantern. "Yes." What had he said about a full moon when they'd first met?

"I think I told you my theory about full moons and women with brown eyes."

She smiled in the dark. "I remember."

"Well?" He looked expectantly at her face. "What do you think? Is it working? Can you read the secrets in my soul?"

The moonlight had turned the world around them black and silver, and when she looked into his eyes, they weren't blue. They were black, black as mystery, black as danger. She stared into their depths, caught by an intangible allure that could draw her in and drown her. She could feel her heart begin to beat a rapid warning in her chest, as though telling her to pull away before it was too late.

But it was already too late. The seduction of her heart was complete. There was no longer any hope of escaping him without being hurt. She knew that.

"What do you see, Pamela?" Michael was whispering. "Tell me what you see."

She was yearning for him to hold her tight, to protect her, but then she realized he was the very thing she needed protection from. She had to do this on her own. It took all her strength to blink quickly, avert her gaze and paste on a tentative smile.

"I see bullfights and teddy bears," she said lightly. "Plus the remnants of a marvelous dinner."

His smile was sardonic. "Then I guess my theory is wrong," he said quietly. "Because that's not what I have inside my soul at all."

She avoided his gaze and began to gather her things. "It's getting late..." she began.

His hand was firm on her chin, forcing her to look him in the eyes. "If I hadn't promised you a cease-fire, Pamela, I'd show you what you're trying to run away from. Next time, I won't be so stupid."

"Michael...."

"We have time. But I'm finding it hard to be patient."

She licked her dry lips. "Perhaps it would be better if you dropped this game," she said softly. "Surely there are other women—"

"Other women!" His laugh was harsh. "I really was wrong about the full moon. I think it's blinded you." He gazed at her, his eyes deep and knowing. "I never really knew what a woman was until I met you," he said slowly, his voice low and husky. "I've had playmates all my life, passing fancies, fun dates. I never even realized there was anything else. Until I met you."

She avoided his eyes, suddenly terrified by his admission. She didn't know what to feel, what to say. This was all too new to her—uncharted territory. And it was dark and she couldn't begin to make out the lay of the land.

"Come on," he said, reaching for the door handle. "I've given you enough to think about tonight." He tilted her chin with his thumb and smiled at her. "But just remember, by the next full moon, I expect you to have opened your eyes a little."

That was all. He walked her to her door and kissed her, his lips softly grazing hers. Then he was gone. But she knew he'd given her another warning, and that she'd be wise to heed it.

PAMELA SPENT HOURS worrying about what he might do when they met again, but she might as well have saved her time and effort. Days passed without another word from him, and then she heard that he was in Japan on a business trip, taking care of some problems on a construction project, and she began to relax. She was a little hurt that he hadn't told her he was going, and actually that he'd gone at all. When he was with her, he acted as though their relationship was his top priority, but he seemed to be able to drop it farther down the list at a moment's notice.

She did get a dozen long-stemmed roses about a week after the dinner in Fresno, but she considered that a feeble effort at best. The card was in Michael's name, but she had a feeling that the handwriting wasn't his.

"Well, how could it be if he's out of the country?" Suzy asked when she brought up her suspicions. "He probably had someone on his staff at White Acres order them for you."

That wasn't good enough, Pamela told herself sulkily. She wanted more. Much more. Probably more than he could give.

Meanwhile, all of Whatley was getting ready for the annual Oktoberfest celebration, held in the middle of October. The streets were roped off and the shops closed as the whole population of the town joined in dancing and feasting through the evening. Started by the merchants as a marketing ploy, it had proved so popular that the original purpose was almost forgotten. It was everyone's holiday now.

"Too bad the resort at White Acres isn't open yet," Mrs. Gimbel, head of the Oktoberfest Committee, lamented when she was in the shop one day, putting posters in the window. "Just think of all the excitement we'll have next year!"

"What you'll have," retorted Jeremy, who happened to be visiting Suzy, "is terrific congestion and a lot of outsiders here to see what they can rip off."

Jeremy had called a meeting to explain his views. Pamela hadn't attended, but she heard it had been a rabble-rousing session and that Jeremy had won a lot of converts on his side.

"Our side," he said when she mentioned it.

"Your side," she said again. "I told you from the start that I wouldn't give you any real support." She shook her head and watched him calmly eating an apple, his eyes on Suzy who was setting up an Indian basket display. "What I don't really understand is what you get out of all this," she said quietly.

He glanced at her, startled. "Me?"

"Yes, you."

He cleared his throat and carefully threw away his apple core in the trash basket nearby. "Did you ever know my father?" he asked.

"No. But Bernice has told me about him."

He shook his head. "He was great. He used to organize protests and really get things done. He got the whole town of Marinbad to boycott lettuce for one whole summer. They loved him." He smiled and shrugged. "If I could stop the White Acres project...if I could do that, all on my own..." He stared into her eyes as though expecting her to understand without any further explanation. "Well, you know what I mean."

She thought she did. He wanted to prove himself to his father. What a strange way to do it. But it was really not her place to criticize his methods or his motives.

So he'd held his meeting and by all accounts, it had been a success. But he'd held it when Michael was out of town. She couldn't help thinking that the results might have been different if Michael had been there.

The day for Oktoberfest seemed charged with a special excitement. By late afternoon, everyone began changing into costumes. Suzy put on a frilly dress with lots of crinolines, and Pamela wore a white peasant blouse with a short green skirt and a tight, brightly embroidered vest.

"Wow," Suzy commented. "That vest makes your waist look tiny. And it sure does push other things out at the top, doesn't it? I wonder who you might be doing that for?"

"It's absolutely authentic," Pamela protested, but she blushed all the same, and they both laughed.

It was in the back of her mind that Michael might show up, but she kept pushing the thought away— partly because she wasn't sure she wanted him to. It would be so much simpler, after all, if he would just disappear from her life. But she knew that wasn't going to happen. There was unfinished business between them. Their relationship wouldn't just fade away. They were building toward something. But she wasn't sure what that something was.

She'd been thinking about the things he'd said the other night. He'd said he wanted her, and Michael Donovan was a man who got what he went after. Why wasn't he trying harder? Was he keeping her off balance on purpose? Did he hope to keep her occupied with worrying over him so she'd have no time or energy left to make waves about White Acres? If that was his plan, it was working, she thought with a crooked smile.

"Philip has brought another woman," Bernice cried, running in to make sure she was the first with the news. "It's that new schoolteacher from Texas."

"Good," Pamela said. "I hope they fall in love."

Bernice and Suzy exchanged a look and Pamela was sure it said, "She's hoping Michael Donovan will show up, poor thing." She countered it with a broad smile. "I'm looking forward to dancing with strangers," she said airily. "I wish we could wear masks. I'd love to have a one-night affair with someone I was never going to see again."

Two mouths dropped as Bernice and Suzy tried to decide whether she was serious. Pamela smiled, feeling a little smug that she'd managed to confound them. "You two go on and start celebrating. I'll close the shop and be along in a few minutes."

She'd planned to stay open until five, as usual, but the street was already buzzing, and it was obvious no one was going to buy Indian artifacts at a time like this. She waved the two women out the door, then closed down the cash register, quickly balanced the books and began securing the store for the night.

The big Russian ducks were still inviting people in. They'd stayed so long that she hardly noticed anymore how incongruous they were with the rest of the shop. The only thing she resented about them now was the chore of carrying them in every night. Stepping outside, she bent down and picked up first one, tucking it under her arm, then another.

"Hello."

The simple word coming from behind her stopped Pamela in her tracks. She recognized the voice immediately and went through a quick sequence of emotions, from elation to pleasure to caution to guarded welcome. And then she turned to face him, a fat duck under each arm.

He was so handsome. He wore a white turtleneck sweater that looked like cashmere and probably was. It emphasized the black curl of his hair and the bright blue of his eyes. The eyes where shimmering with amusement. "Going to market?" he asked, gesturing at the ducks. She could see reflected in his eyes what a picture she must make in her peasant garb, with her livestock in hand.

Suddenly she was laughing. Regardless of everything else, she was so happy to see him. "To market, to market, to buy a fat duck," she agreed. She plopped the two she was holding into his arms. "Here, you can help carry these while I get the others."

He looked from one ceramic duck to the other, amused. "Interesting," he murmured as he carried them into the store.

"Yes, aren't they?" she said, following him with two more. "Suzy bought them one day while I was out, and they've kind of taken over."

They set down the ducks and turned to face each other. "I—I just have a few more things to do before I close," she said and escaped behind the counter. She locked the safe and put away the ledger, watching Michael out of the corner of her eye. He was looking over her shop, slowly moving past each display, studying each detail. Though he'd stopped in often during the past few weeks, he hadn't really had a chance to examine the new arrangement. It was very different from when he'd last seen it a month or so earlier. Two of the sections were almost complete. The Indian display was set up like a camp scene, with baskets and utensils strewn about as though a Miwok family had just left them. Next was a scene from Spanish California, designed to give customers the impression of entering the courtyard of a hacienda. Silver buttons, lace, ribbons, antique spurs, pictures of horses and fandangos, and antique jewelry were set out in lacquer boxes as though the lady of the house were doing a bit of spring housecleaning.

The mountain-man section should have come next, but Pamela hadn't quite decided how to approach it. So she'd gone ahead and begun the Gold Rush, filling the area with lovely rocks and minerals, gold-panning equipment and posters from those wild days. This was the display that seemed to interest Michael most. She watched as he picked up a sparkling geode, and then a large grouping of amethyst crystals.

"That just about does it," she said at last, coming out from behind the counter. "One of these days I'm going to train the ducks to close up by themselves and then we can all retire." He walked toward her, smiling, and she expected him to comment on the changes she'd made in the shop, but he didn't say a word.

Instead, he stopped very close and looked down at her. "Will you come with me to Oktoberfest?" he asked with almost formal politeness.

"I don't know, mister," she said, head to the side, teasing him just a little. "That's a pretty drastic step.

I mean, going to Oktoberfest together. People will talk.''

"Let them talk,'' he said, taking her face between his hands and smiling into her eyes. "We have better things on our minds.'' His kiss was sweet but spiced with promise, and she found herself clinging to his lips even as he was drawing back. He grinned at her. "Save that thought,'' he said. "We're going to need it later.''

They walked out onto the street and it was like entering a huge amusement park. Traffic had been blocked off and carnival stands had been erected up and down the sidewalks. A huge organ stood at one end of town, its music booming through the air. Townspeople had all been transformed into German country-folk with their lederhosen and embroidered vests. Pamela laughed in delight and when Michael curved his arm around her shoulders to lead her through the crowd, she smiled at him and didn't pull away.

"Hey!'' A man named Jake whom she'd known in high school and who now owned a lumberyard stopped them with a shout. "You can't get into the spirit without these!'' He thrust mugs of beer into their hands, and it turned out that Michael knew him, too.

"*Ja, prosit!*'' they cried, raising their mugs high and laughing.

"Be sure to try the sausage table,'' Jake urged them. "My wife is doing the cooking and she's a pro.''

An oom-pah band began to play, and couples danced in the street. Michael and Pamela pushed on, watching everything, holding tightly together, not saying much but communicating all the same.

They paused at a corner just as a huge horse-drawn wagon full of hay was going by. "Pamela!" Bernice and Fred were on board, waving frantically. "Come on up! We're going for a hayride!"

The wagon slowed but Michael whispered, "Let's not. I want you to myself." And she felt warm.

"Come on—hurry!" Bernice called as the wagon began to pick up speed again.

"Pretend you didn't understand," Michael whispered, grinning, and they both waved and smiled and watched as Bernice and Fred rode out of sight.

They found a stage set up for acrobats, and a beauty contest for five-year-olds. They sampled sausages from steaming tables, sauerkraut, potato salad, rye bread and apple strudel. They watched German couples doing the "Chicken Dance" and then Pamela actually got Michael to try a polka.

Michael doing a polka. She would never have imagined such a thing even a few hours earlier. But with the oom-pah band playing and everyone joining in, it seemed only natural. And it was only natural that he managed to look terrific doing it.

"You're good," she cried as they bounced down the street, arm in arm, dancing to the rollicking music.

"Of course," he told her with a shrug. "I could have told you that." And his eyes said he meant at more than dancing.

The high-school band marched through, followed by the cheerleaders and the football team. Since it was football season, they were hailed as heroes. Pamela and Michael wandered through the streets, looking in store windows, laughing at the children, watching the others having fun. They spoke to those they knew, but never for long. They wanted to be with each other, and everyone they met seemed to sense that. As the night grew later, they found themselves alone at the far end of the park, the lights and crowds far behind them.

"What's that?" Michael asked, pointing to a black shimmer just visible through the trees.

"That's the fountain," she told him. "I guess they turned it on for Oktoberfest."

They walked toward it until they reached the high, rounded sides. Even in the dark they could see the coins glistening at the bottom.

"A wishing fountain?" Michael asked.

"Yes."

He took out a coin. "What shall we wish for?"

She recalled how they'd met at the old wishing well on White Acres and wondered if he remembered, too. That had been such a magic day. She'd felt as though she were floating on an enchanted cloud, as though she'd left the cares and troubles of her world far behind. There was a little of that feeling tonight. Maybe it was part of Michael's charm, she thought dreamily. Maybe he carried that cloud with him and could snap his fingers and make it appear whenever he needed it. "Let's wish for rain," she said spontaneously.

"What?" He turned to her, amused. "Why rain?"

Good question. She groped for an answer. "Because we haven't had any yet this fall, and if we don't soon, there are going to be forest fires."

He held the silver coin in his hand, considering. "I was thinking of something a little more personal," he said.

She hesitated, looking down into the water. The sound of the happy crowd seemed far away. Anything more personal was dangerous. "Wishes don't work, anyway," she murmured. "I've made a hundred wishes that never panned out."

He was silent and she wondered if he was remembering what he'd said when they first met, what he'd promised. "Tell me all your wishes," he'd said, "and I'll make them come true."

"I don't think I dare," she'd told him honestly.

"Nothing ventured, nothing gained," he'd said.

Was she still too wary to trust him? Maybe not. Maybe tonight...

"I believe in wishes," he said at last, and she looked up in surprise because emotion in his voice told her he meant what he was saying. "They work for me." He was quiet for a moment, then he threw the coin into the center of the fountain. "There," he said. "Now we'll see who's right."

She had to smile at his pleased expression. "What did you wish for?" she asked.

"Uh-uh." He shook a finger at her. "You know I can't tell you that."

"Let me guess." She smiled up at him as he came closer. She knew he was going to take her in his arms and kiss her and she was ready. It was an enchanted time, just as all the other times with Michael had been. How wonderful if they could stay in this fantasy world, but she knew reality would come stealing back the next day.

Until then, she wanted to enjoy him. "You wished for a new Ferrari, only black this time, so you'd have one for every mood."

He placed his hands on the sides of her head and gazed down, his mood teasing. "You're so cold," he told her cheerfully, "you might as well be in Alaska."

She chuckled, knowing he meant only that her guess was far off the mark. "Hmm," she murmured as he drew her in to snuggle against his chest. "Maybe you're hoping someone will give you a Lear jet for Christmas?" She grinned. "If you are, don't look at me."

He tipped up her face and began kissing the tender area just in front of her ear. "Something much more precious than that," he whispered between kisses.

Her knees were growing weak. She raised her arms and linked them behind his head, partly to hold herself up. "I'll bet you're dying for one of my fat Russian ducks, aren't you?" she breathed, her head beginning to spin. "I just might be able to accommodate you there."

He laughed softly, pushing her hair back and beginning a sensuous examination of her neck. "More precious even than that," he growled, pulling her close and looking down into her face. There was a strange light shining in his eyes, and it make her tremble. She wanted to look away, but she couldn't. He frightened her and yet she needed him so badly.

"Tell me what it is," she whispered, more to keep the conversation going and to postpone the inevitable than to find an answer. "just one word. A hint." He dropped a quick kiss on her lips, then stared into her eyes again. "What did you wish for?" she asked one last time.

His gaze was a swirling autumn storm, dark and unpredictable. The light from the center of town formed changing shadows across his face, each flicker making him seem almost a different person. With each change of the light, his face looked hard, then soft, showing strength and gentleness by turns. His hands tightened on her shoulders, and he pulled her even closer, muttering a single word just before his lips came down on hers, beginning a fiery kiss that sent her senses reeling.

Love. Had that been the word? No, it couldn't have been. Michael wouldn't have wished for something like that. The whole idea was ridiculous. Michael was a man of wealth and power, a man who dealt in things that could be bought and controlled. Love was a slippery intangible. It didn't depend on the things that were important to Michael. It was against his nature to need it, want it.

His kiss deepened and she lost her train of thought as she responded, opening to him as she'd never opened to a man before, leaving herself vulnerable. She loved him. There was no use trying to hide that from herself any longer. The feel of his smooth skin, the scent of his breath, the sweet, sweet taste of him, seemed to fill her senses, intoxicating her. But there was more than that.

She loved his handsome face, and yes, his body and the incomparable way it made her feel. But even more, she loved the man. She loved the way he walked, the way one eyebrow rose when he had a question. She loved the toughness she could feel in him, and the little-boy sweetness that occasionally surfaced. She loved the way he kissed her, as though she were someone dear and special, someone to be treated with care. She loved him more than any man she'd ever known. She might even love him enough to forget her doubts and resentments, and to start fresh. She was almost ready to, if he said the right words.

Could he feel it? Could he tell from her kiss, from her surrender? She wasn't sure. And she wasn't sure if this was the right time to let him know. She only knew her body was his, and her heart could be, too.

A one-night affair with a stranger—that was what she'd told Bernice and Suzy she wanted. But she'd been wrong. What would really please her was something long term—with Michael. She wanted to be his. She wanted him to be hers. But could that really happen? Did Michael give? Or did he only take what he wanted and move on?

His breath was ragged as he drew back, looked at her, then hugged her close again. She could feel the wildness of his heartbeat. "You are so soft and beautiful in the moonlight," he told her huskily. "You make me feel drunk."

She pressed her face to his chest, letting his heart pound against her cheek. "Me, too," she whispered.

"We'd better get back," he said gruffly, and she thrilled to the thought that her kiss had brought him close to losing control. If she said, "No, let's stay," what would happen? If she said, "Come back to my apartment with me..." Excitement chased fear through her bloodstream and she shivered. She wanted him so badly—she wanted to tell him so. But no. Not yet. It wasn't the time.

"All right," she agreed, and was pleased to hear a steadiness in her own voice that belied the excitement raging beneath. Her blood was on fire and she could hardly stand, but she sounded as cool as ever.

They walked slowly back toward the lights, arm in arm. The warmth of his body was her protection, her shield. She was a woman in love, and she knew it. She'd found the man of her dreams.

As they entered the busy street, she felt Michael tense almost imperceptibly and she looked up to see what had caused his reaction. Jeremy and Suzy were coming toward them along the sidewalk. Pamela managed a smile even though she felt almost too dreamy for conversation.

"Hi, there," she said as they came face-to-face. She ignored Suzy's wide-eyed stare as she took in the closeness between Pamela and Michael. "Are you two enjoying Oktoberfest?"

Suzy nodded, but Jeremy was frowning. He'd noticed the closeness, too, and was obviously affronted. "By hook or by crook, huh, Donovan?" he said acidly.

Michael sighed. "Let's not get into it now, Jeremy," he said in bored tone.

"Why not?" the younger man challenged. "Isn't that what you're doing? Using the evening as a choice opportunity for co-opting your opponent?"

Time seemed to stand still for Pamela. Jeremy rushed on, saying, "You think you can charm Pamela into thinking you have a right to ruin White Acres by turning it into a tourist trap. You think just because she's a soft touch you've got her twisted around your finger. You think you can buy her just like—"

Suddenly Michael turned from a charming companion to a rock-hard combatant, his body tense, his eyes flashing with barely leashed fury, as he said with cold deadly calm, "You can say what you want about me, Keaton, but leave Pamela out of it, if you don't want to face the consequences."

Jeremy's face went white. He swallowed hard, but couldn't force out any words.

Michael's smile was coldly triumphant. "That's better," he said icily. "Reticence becomes you. You ought to try it more often."

And then they were walking along the street again, Michael's arm around Pamela just as it had been before. But everything had changed.

They drank another mug of beer and watched the folk dancing. Michael smiled at her, and she snuggled against him. But the magic had gone out of the evening. Jeremy had broken the spell, and Pamela had to face reality again.

She was in love with Michael. That would never change. But she shouldn't be. It was wrong, foolish. It was doomed from the start.

What did they have, after all? She knew he was attracted to her, but beyond that, she had no idea how he felt. He'd held back the truth from her before. He'd made her fall in love under false pretenses. Even if he told her he loved her, could she trust him? And could Jeremy be right? After all, the first time she'd seen Michael he'd been sizing up her property. Making a success at White Acres was obviously very important to him. Might he not find it convenient to use her again?

She didn't like these ugly thoughts. They hurt, and they made the rest of the world seem sordid. When she looked into Michael's clear blue eyes, she couldn't believe he'd do anything to harm her. But when she stood back and tried to be objective...

She shivered again.

"Are you cold?"

"Not really. But I think it's about time I went home."

He could sense the new distance between them, and he didn't argue. He walked with her to the shop and she turned away from him when they reached the bottom of the stairs. He might expect her to invite him up, but she wasn't going to. She had no more thoughts of affairs with strangers. That was part of the fantasy world Michael could create so easily—the world Jeremy had punctured with his accusing words.

"Will you be going away again?" she asked.

He raised an eyebrow. "Going where?"

She shrugged. "I heard you were in Japan."

"Oh." He smiled. "No, I won't be going to Japan. But I will have to fly to Seattle in the morning, and I might be gone for a few days."

She took a deep breath and then got it out all at once. "Is Jeremy right?" she asked shakily. "Are you using me?"

His face hardened and he stared down at her for a long moment before he replied. "Is that what you think?" he said, his voice soft but deadly.

She shrugged, indicating her helplessness. "There is quite a bit of evidence—" she began, but he cut her off with an oath.

"Evidence! I don't want to hear about evidence." He took her chin in his hand, tilting her face toward his. "I want to hear what you think, what you believe, what's in your heart."

She was shivering uncontrollably now. He frightened her. Not because she feared physical violence— she knew he wouldn't hurt her that way. But what she felt for him was so strong, and he could so easily turn it against her.

"I—I don't know...."

His eyes were flaming with anger. "You don't know. And yet you accuse me of being the worst kind of criminal. Why, Pamela? What have I done to deserve that?"

She closed her eyes, steeling herself, then opened them to stare into his fury again. "You lied to me," she said firmly. "You didn't tell me who you were when you first came. And then you let me think you...came back for me, when all the while you'd forgotten all about me."

"Forgotten you?" His smile was humorless and his fingers tightened on her chin. "Never."

She was growing stronger now, and she held his gaze. "Then why did you do it?" she demanded.

He frowned slightly as though searching for the reason himself. "Maybe it's because I want it all, Pamela," he said huskily. His hand slipping down to cup the throbbing pulse at the base of her throat. "I want White Acres. I want you."

"And you'll do anything to get what you want?" she asked breathlessly, heart racing.

"Yes," he answered, his mouth twisting almost cruelly. "Anything." He gripped her shoulders with savage emphasis. "Anything, Pamela."

His kiss was hot and urgent, and she could feel the relentless fire of his passion as its flames licked at her resolve. He took her mouth with a hunger that made her gasp, but it coaxed an answering flame in her, and she felt weak with longing when he drew away. "I'll even give you time, Pamela," he said, his blue gaze searching for the truth behind her dazed eyes. "Time to come to grips with me and what I'm going to demand of you. And that's the most difficult gift I've ever given anyone."

His smile was ruthless as he let her go. "So you see, darling, it doesn't matter much whether I lied before. I'd lie, or cheat, or steal, or do anything else you could think of to have you. You might as well resign yourself to your fate."

She was speechless and he gazed at her for a few moments more, as though memorizing every curve and angle of her face. "I'll see you in a few days then," he said huskily, bending and kissing her lips so softly she hardly knew he was there. And then he was gone, striding off down the street toward, she assumed, wherever he'd parked his car. And she was filled with a terrified yearning that threatened to choke her.

CHAPTER EIGHT

IF ONLY SHE COULD FIND a few hours to sort things out, Pamela kept thinking, she might have made sense of all this confusion.

But she didn't get a second, let alone hours. Merchandise she'd ordered with the last of the money from the sale of White Acres was continually arriving at the door, and she stayed up late into the night trying to arrange it in some form that stayed true to the plan she'd devised.

In a way, she was thankful for the frantic busyness. At least the days sped by—days during which she heard nothing from Michael. If it hadn't been for her work she would have spent the time staring at the telephone and wondering if she really wanted it to ring.

Instead she was dragging crates across the floor and calling out instructions to Suzy. "No, that soap's just like the type they made at the old missions. Put it in the Spanish section."

"I wonder what kind of bathrooms they had back then?" Suzy mused as she did what she'd been told.

"Don't ask," Pamela advised. "You really don't want to know."

She'd made a semipeace with Jeremy. Suzy had asked him to come to the shop the morning after Oktoberfest to apologize to her, and she'd accepted.

"I'm not your martyr, you know," she told him. "If you want to fight what Michael is doing at White Acres, go right ahead. But don't do it in my name."

She could see by the thinning of his lips that he thought she'd gone over to the side of the enemy, but if he was honest with himself he'd have to admit she'd never told him she wanted him to stop Michael. Not ever.

He and Suzy were still seeing a lot of each other. Pamela wondered now and then if she ought to encourage Suzy to see some of her old friends, too. But then she remembered how little she'd been inclined to take that sort of advice at Suzy's age, and she refrained. After all, who was she to be giving advice on love affairs?

Seven days passed before she heard anything from Michael, and then it was in the form of a small package that arrived in the mail. She ripped open the brown paper with trembling hands and cursed herself for her excitement. Inside the little box was a felt bag with a drawstring. She pulled it open and out spilled six small gold nuggets.

"Dear Pamela," the enclosed note said, "please take these for your Gold Rush display. I found them when I was panning on your river last Spring. They look like teardrops, don't they? I'll be back in a few days. Wait for me. Michael."

Teardrops. Tears of gold. She took them up in her hand and tried to look at them, but the tears in her own eyes got in the way and the warm gold color swam and blended into the other colors of the room. She blinked hard. She wasn't going to cry, for heaven's sake. She wasn't a weeper. Except for that one episode the day she'd signed away White Acres, she hadn't cried in years. Even when her father died, the crying had been minimal. There'd been too much to do, too many things to consider. She'd had no time to cry. And now here she was, dewy-eyed over a few gold nuggets. She was only grateful there was no one else in the shop to see her.

She hadn't the slightest idea why she was getting so emotional. It had something to do with Michael—and loving him. Beyond that, she didn't want to delve. She tried to thrust the incident into the back of her mind.

She put the nuggets in a small pan and placed them high on a shelf where they could be seen but not touched. She left them there for almost an hour before fetching a ladder and climbing up to retrieve them. She replaced them in the felt pouch and put that in the pocket of her skirt, which she would gently pat from time to time. She wasn't sure why, but she found it comforting to feel the little nuggets there. Perhaps they were a link, these tears of gold, between what she and Michael were today and the spellbound strangers they'd been that afternoon on her hill, and she wanted to keep them close as a remembrance. She told herself she'd return them to the display in a day or two.

She got another surprise later that day. Mr. Scofield, the pharmacist next door, dropped by, waving a piece of poorly printed red paper. "You going to the meeting?" he asked, thrusting the pamphlet in her face. "That Jeremy Keaton is creating quite a stir, isn't he?"

"Yes, he is," she said, taking the red pamphlet and lowering it a bit so she could read it, "and no, I'm not." She looked at the paper. It was covered with Jeremy's rantings. There were examples of towns that had let development carry them to ruin, and examples of towns that had fought the developer and were now islands of tranquillity in a tumultuous world. There were lists of points against the White Acres resort, and lists of people who backed the good cause. But most important, there was a photograph of Pamela.

It was just a photograph. And below, the caption said only, "Pamela Starbuck, last in the line that created White Acres out of the wilderness, forced to give up her heritage to Miracle Development."

It didn't say she backed Jeremy. It didn't say he was doing all this in her name. But the implication was clear.

"These are all over town." Mr. Scofield told her. "Everyone's seen it. And just about everyone's planning to go to the big meeting next week."

She'd been against the new resort from the first, but she wasn't about to come out and fight Michael publicly, especially now that she'd finally admitted to herself that she loved him. Jeremy knew she refused to go along with his campaign, and yet he'd put her in this position. She was furious.

Pamela stormed through the town until she found Suzy at the library, browsing through college catalogs. "Did you know about this?" she flared, backing her up against the shelves.

Suzy looked very guilty. "I told him not to use your picture. I'm sorry, Pam—he just thinks this is so important...."

"I suppose you supplied him with the photo."

She nodded miserably. "That was before I knew what he meant to do with it."

"Where is Jeremy?"

She looked even more guilty. "He went to get advice from some friends in Berkeley. He won't be back for a couple of days."

"Great. Meanwhile, what am I supposed to do? Go around to everyone in town and explain to each one that my picture is on this piece of propaganda by mistake?"

Behind her anger was the fear of what Michael would think when he saw it, as she was sure he would. Why hadn't she been open with him? Why hadn't they discussed the issue of where she stood and cleared the air? Instead, they'd both tiptoed around it as though it would explode in their faces if they touched it. Anything she said now would sound like an excuse. How she would love to wring Jeremy's neck!

Her rage at Jeremy would have to simmer until he got back, but the pamphlet did give rise to another incident. Now that Oktoberfest was over, Mrs. Gimbel was involved in the town meeting that was being called, thanks to Jeremy's instigations, to discuss the White Acres development.

She came into the shop one afternoon and raved about all the imaginative changes Pamela had made. "It's wonderful," she said. "You'll put us into all the guidebooks with this."

"Everyone seems to like it," Pamela agreed. "But I can't say too many sales have followed the acclaim." She was having a particularly wearing day and her usually bright spirits were flagging. "I've put every last penny into the inventory. If sales don't take off soon..." Her voice trailed off. She certainly didn't mean to complain, especially not to Mrs. Gimbel, one of the town's civic leaders. "But Suzy and I are having a wonderful time with the renovation,'' she said quickly.

"I'm sure you are," Mrs. Gimbel said absently. She was staring at the ducks. "Do they have names?" she whispered, as though they might overhear and be offended.

"Not yet," said Pamela hiding a smile. "But you're welcome to name one, if you wish."

Mrs. Gimbel walked over and stared at the largest duck. The red bandana almost covered its beady little eyes, but some contact seemed to spring up between the two of them.

"Petrushka," Mrs. Gimbel said decisively, touching the duck with her foot. When she turned back, her face was all business. "Now, dear, about White Acres."

Pamela had no further problem with smiles. "What about White Acres?"

"We want to make sure we cover all the angles," Mrs. Gimbel said. "We've formed a committee to go out and take a look at Michael Donovan's development. The committee will report on its findings at the town meeting. The Miracle people invited us to come on Thursday at eleven, and they'll even feed us lunch." She paused, smiling at Pamela. "We want you on that committee."

"Me?" Pamela's heart sank. She didn't want to do it. It was bad enough that she'd been dragged into the center of the controversy by Jeremy's pamphlet. Besides, she knew it would be painful to see what they were doing to her old home. "If you're asking me because of that pamphlet..."

"No, dear," Mrs. Gimbel assured her. "We have two members who are for the development, two

against, and then there's me. I'm totally neutral.'' She
reached for Pamela's hand. ''To a lot of people in this
town, you're still White Acres, Pamela. It would mean
a lot to us all to get your opinion.''

So she agreed, and when Mrs. Gimbel left, she had
Petrushka under her arm, and there were only five
ducks left waddling in front of Pamela's store.

By the next afternoon, there were only four. Mrs.
Van Orden had seen Mrs. Gimbel's duck and wanted
one of her own. ''Mine's named Olga,'' she said
proudly as she carried her new charge from the store.
A sale was a sale, but Pamela felt a little sad to see it
go.

Thursday came much too quickly. The committee
met at Mrs. Gimbel's house and traveled to White
Acres in two cars. Pamela was quiet, her mind racing
with conflicting emotions. She hadn't been out this
way since early summer. She knew there would be
changes. She was prepared for that. But now she was
about to come face-to-face with them, and she wasn't
sure how she would react.

The trees were a palette of colors, reds and oranges
and yellows mixed with the evergreens. The ones that
had already lost their leaves presented a stark and jarring contrast to the lush vegetation. An omen, she
thought somewhat irrationally as she looked at a grove
of aspen standing straight and bare in the morning
sunlight. Funny. She'd always loved the fall, yet this
year it seemed so sad.

''Here we are,'' Mrs. Gimbel announced breezily as
they pulled in through the high white gates, and Pamela felt a lump growing in her throat. She noticed
pickets just off the land.

"Oh, those strikers," Mrs. Gimbel said. "It's the stonemasons. They want more time off. If they don't watch out, Michael will hire replacements and give them all the time off they could ever want."

But Pamela's emotional state was too great for her to pay much attention. She was going home, only it wasn't home anymore. She wasn't sure she should have done this.

She looked hungrily at it all as they took the long drive to the house. There was the old black oak tree where she'd hidden her box of treasures when she was seven; there was the rickety storage shack she and her friends had used for playing school; there were the portable beehives. It gave her a momentary lift to see that those remnants of her past hadn't been removed. But as they drove up, she made a point of not looking toward the place where the cemetery had been. The model had shown new stables placed on that very site, and she couldn't bear to think of it, let alone see it done. The thought of those beloved names, those weathered headstones, crushed to dust beneath a building meant for the pleasures of rich tourists made her feel slightly sick. If she looked and actually saw it, she didn't know what she might do.

Because there were changes. Lots of them. As they arrived at the house, she gazed in wonder at all the changes Miracle Development was bringing about.

The tall colonial mansion her ancestors had built still dominated the landscape, but there was a flurry of building going on around it. Single-story structures were scattered across what had once been the family orchard, and down the hill, toward the river. A few of them were completed. Painted white, they looked like miniature versions of her house. Workers were busy planting trees and shrubbery around each cottage. And because a lot of the trees had been left standing, the scene avoided the bare, immature look so many of these developments had at first. There was no use avoiding the truth. It was going to be lovely.

That was what she kept telling herself as they were shown through a model bungalow and then around the grounds. It was going to be lovely. But it wasn't White Acres.

She felt strangely detached as they took their tour— as though she were watching from high above. This wasn't her old home. This was something completely new, something that had no bearing on her life. It couldn't touch her, not really.

Then why did she feel so cold, no numb? Why was there a faint buzzing in her ears? Suddenly she understood. These new cottages really didn't affect her, but she dreaded going into the big house. She didn't think she could bear it if they'd changed things inside her mother's house.

The Miracle Development people brought out little electric golf carts and drove them past the wishing well on their way to see the golf course. She had to smile when she noticed that the fake wishing well was still there. Had Michael spared it with her in mind? But not for long, she was sure. It looked much too worn and crumbling to go with the bright new sparkle her land was taking on.

They were driven to the river and shown where the dock was going to be, where the rafting would take place, and they looked at the plans for the restaurant that would be situated at the water's edge. And then they turned back toward the house, and Pamela went cold again.

CHAPTER NINE

SHE WONDERED if Michael was in the house. She hadn't heard anything from him, except for the gold nuggets, since Oktoberfest.

"Mr. Donovan is away," their guide said, as though reading her thoughts. His name was Bob, and she knew he was one of Michael's top assistants. "He asked me to make his apologies for not being here to greet you himself, but he had business in Los Angeles."

Japan, Seattle, Los Angeles. Wasn't the man ever home? Pamela stepped out of the cart and stood looking up at the wide entryway she'd run through so many times. It yawned before her now, mysterious and frightening.

"Please come in."

She couldn't take the first step and Mrs. Gimbel, seeing her distress, grasped her arm and led her in. "Come on, Pamela," she whispered cheerfully. "Your mother was one of my best friends. I'm sure she'd want her daughter keeping an eye on her house for her, even if it has been sold."

The buzzing in her ears grew louder, but she made it into the house. Standing in the entryway, she slowly turned and looked into the living room, the dining room, the hallway to the den and library. Something was wrong. Everything looked just as it had when she'd lived there. She stood motionless for a moment, and then dashed from one room to the next. Yes, it was true. Same furniture, same paintings, same placement of flower arrangements. Everything was just the same, except...except better. The wood had been restored to the way it had looked years before. The walls had been painted, the draperies copied with new material. Everything sparkled and shone like new. But it was just the same.

She was shaken, not knowing whether to be pleased or horrified. She'd been prepared for changes, prepared to be hurt by them. She'd been ready for that. But this...she wasn't sure what to make of it. In a sense this was almost worse than if she'd walked in and found her house filled with glass-and-chrome furniture. The echoes of her past still filled the rooms. No one had any right to those echoes. No one but Pamela and Suzy.

They sat down in the dining room, at the same table her family had used, to eat a wonderful lunch of shrimp and straw-mushroom salad in ginger dressing, served with cheese bread and avocado.

"Is the chef already in residence?" Mrs. Gimbel wanted to know.

"No," Bob replied. "Actually, we have a cook who handles meals for the workers who stay here, but Mr. Donovan had a chef from one of the other Miracle projects flown in just for today. He wanted you to experience the quality of cuisine that will be served here."

And experience it they did. The food was truly delicious. But as the others lingered over coffee, Pamela excused herself, ostensibly to visit the bathroom, but actually to go exploring.

The ground floor had been kept so much the same that she had to see what had been done upstairs. She left the dining room and walked toward the bathroom, stopped at the door and looked quickly around to make sure the coast was clear, then turned to run up the stairs instead.

The banister had been refinished, the stairs recarpeted. At the top of the stairs stood a low table set with fresh flowers. That was new. And very nice. She turned toward her own bedroom. Her hand shook as she reached for the knob. Of course it was going to be different. Of course she was going to be horrified. But she had to see.

She threw the door open and stepped inside. She slowly paced the room, looking in every corner. All her personal things were gone, but everything else was the same. The matching bedspread and curtains she'd chosen only a few years ago still cheered the room with their bright yellows and oranges.

"If I brought back my clothes and pictures," she whispered to herself, "it would be exactly as it was."

Why hadn't Michael changed the room? Or perhaps, she reminded herself, he just hadn't changed it yet. Why did he need all these bedrooms if he was building the cottages for his visitors?

Back in the hall she looked toward the master bedroom, the room where her parents had slept. Michael must be using that for his own. She walked quickly to the door and opened it, peering in. No. That, too, looked just the same.

She frowned and hurried toward the corner bedroom they'd always called the Blue Room. That was the only other room big enough to hold a man like Michael. All hesitation was gone now. She didn't give a thought to the fact that she was trespassing on someone else's property. She pushed open the door to the Blue Room and sure enough, that was the one Michael was using.

It had been the best guest room when she'd lived there, with its enchanting view of the river and the mountains. They'd always saved it for very special guests. The blue theme was still carried out in the wallpaper and bedspread, but both were new and very lush looking. The window treatment was different. Blue thin-bladed blinds hung where frilly curtains had once fluttered. For the rest, the furniture was the same. But Michael was there, everywhere in the room. She could sense his presence, even though she knew he was hundreds of miles away.

Michael—her willful, ruthless love. She had to admit he was building a beautiful resort on her land. It hurt to see the changes, and yet she knew she could learn to live with them. But could she learn to live with Michael's amoral nature? He had the instincts of a pirate, the scruples of a buccaneer. She loved him, but he terrified her.

She went to the closet and slid open the door. The clothes were Michael's. Reaching in, she took a shirt in her hands and brought it to her face, closing her eyes and breathing in the clean, fresh smell of newly laundered cloth. And of Michael.

Affection grew in her as she stood among his things, grew until she felt she would burst with it. She ran her hand across the fabric of his suit coat, the furriness of a sweater, and she felt she was almost touching him.

There was a muffled shout from downstairs and a burst of laughter, and she knew she should return to the others. Closing the closet door, she started toward the door. But she couldn't leave. Not quite yet. Without letting herself think about what she was doing, she walked to the bed, folded back the spread and touched the fluffy white pillow. His pillow. The feeling overwhelmed her and she sat down on the bed, spreading her hands across the fabric of the cover, luxuriating in loving him.

A sound in the hall whipped her head around but she didn't have time to move before Michael appeared in the doorway. He was carrying a suitcase in one hand, a briefcase in the other. His tie was pulled loose and the top buttons of his shirt were open. His tumbled hair and bloodshot eyes suggested that he hadn't slept in a few nights. But when he saw her, he smiled.

"You see," he said softly. "I told you my wishes always come true." And he entered the room, kicking the door closed behind him.

Pamela was almost too stunned to be embarrassed. "I—I..." She jumped up from the bed and looked wildly around for a good excuse to explain her presence in his bedroom.

"Hush." He dropped his bags and came quickly to her, putting a finger to her lips. "Don't tell me the truth. I don't want to hear logic. If you only came to sweep the dust devils out from under my bed, I don't want to know." He dropped a soft kiss on her lips. "Let me believe you came because you couldn't stay away," he whispered huskily. "I like that so much better."

He was half teasing, but as he kissed her again, more deeply and more thoroughly, she sensed the seriousness beneath the jest. "I'm just exploring," she told him breathlessly when he gave her a chance. "I'm here with a committee—"

"Yes, I know. I saw them downstairs."

"And I wanted to see what you'd done with the rooms...."

His smile looked tired. "You're welcome in my room anytime." But he drew away from her, shrugging out of his suit jacket and tossing it onto a chair.

"How was Los Angeles?" She knew she should leave, but somehow she couldn't. While he was removing his coat she surreptitiously covered his pillow again, but he turned and caught her at it. She straightened quickly and he grinned but made no comment, other than to answer her question.

"How was Los Angeles?" He grimaced. "Who knows? I was in a basement room in the midst of labor negotiations the whole time I was there. I never saw the sun."

"You didn't drive home after that?"

He shook his head. "I flew into Fresno and drove from there." He ran a hand through his hair, rumpling it even more. "I haven't slept for at least forty-eight hours."

She felt a deep pang of sympathy and started toward the door. "Oh, I'll get out of here so you can get some rest."

He put out a hand to stop her. "Don't go," he said softly. "Stay a little longer." His grin was bittersweet. "You don't have to worry. I haven't the strength to threaten your virtue right now."

His hand curved around her neck caressingly and she couldn't resist. "Would you...would you like me to rub your back?" she offered tentatively.

Flexing his shoulders, he began to unbutton his shirt. "If I'd thought, I would have wished for that, too," he murmured. "You see? My wishes are even getting ahead of me now."

She was already regretting her impulsive suggestion. She'd never given anyone a back rub before and she wasn't sure how to go about it. Did one pat and stroke, or push and pound? He was taking off his shirt. That must mean he expected her to touch his bare flesh. She hadn't thought of that. What had seemed so simple when she'd brought it up had suddenly become awfully complicated.

"Are you going to lie down or..." she began awkwardly, gesturing vaguely.

He smiled at her, his eyes heavy lidded. "It's just about at the point of lie down or fall down," he said. "Right here, okay?" He flopped onto the bed, facedown, and she dropped beside him, reaching hesitantly to touch his back.

He sighed and closed his eyes. She began to rub, using only one hand at first, then both, working hard at his tired muscles, then stroking softly to soothe them, and once she'd begun she had no more doubts. The sense of what he needed seemed to come naturally to her.

"That's wonderful," he murmured drowsily. "Keep it up."

She smiled, ridiculously happy at having pleased him with such a simple thing. She was actually enjoying this. It was a bit like kneading bread dough. Only better. Much, much better.

His skin was butter smooth and deeply tanned. As her hands worked over him she could feel the sheathed movement of the steel underneath. The play of muscle against muscle was beautiful to see. She wanted to lean down and kiss him between the shoulder blades, but she forced herself to wait.

"Right there," he said suddenly, stretching his neck as her hands touched the tense muscles at the base. "Harder. Really give it to me."

She worked the flesh harder and he sighed with relaxed gratification. "Mrs. Gimbel may not have had this sort of thing in mind for you when she got you on the committee," he said. "But I'm glad you came."

"The committee!" Her hands stopped and she sat up, aghast. How could she have forgotten them for this long?

"Don't worry," he said huskily, his eyes still closed. "They went out to see the stables. They were leaving when I arrived. They'll just think you're wandering around the grounds somewhere."

She touched him again, glorying in the smooth beauty of his back. It was exciting to have him like this, as though she'd tamed a panther to her hand. He exuded a sense of leashed danger just barely under control. One wrong move...

"What does your committee think so far?" he asked.

"We haven't really discussed it together. I imagine we'll do that when we get back to town." She hesitated. "Michael, I'm...well, this business about Jeremy..." She wasn't sure what she wanted to say—that she accepted the changes at White Acres, perhaps, or that she was sorry Jeremy was making things difficult.

"Forget it." His response was cryptic and she started to object, but he continued. "I understand Jeremy. He and I are a lot alike in some ways."

"What?" She almost laughed aloud. There was nothing similar between them!

"No, we are. I understand his motivations." His voice hardened and at the same time she could feel a hardening in the muscles of his back. "But this time, he's got to lose. Because I'm not going to give up White Acres."

She was struck by the intensity in his voice. "Is it really so important to you?" she asked.

"Yes. For a lot of reasons." He moved under her hand. "We lost a similar resort plan in Oregon a few years ago. In a little town called Yellowfin. Environmentalists turned the town around, and I let them do it." He shifted, and she was almost afraid to reach for him again. There was a flame of anger in him now. "It won't happen again. I won't let anyone take this away from me."

She believed him. And she was glad she wasn't the one trying to stop him. Had he seen the pamphlet Jeremy had put out? Perhaps she should tell him about it.

But before she got a chance, he was rolling over on his back and pulling her down onto his bare chest. "Stay with me, Pamela," he murmured huskily, hugging her close. "I want to always find you here on my bed when I come home."

She wasn't sure if he was serious or just indulging in light wishes, but she snuggled against him as though she'd finally found a home.

There was a sudden noise from the hall and they both went very still, listening.

Mrs. Gimbel's voice came to them clearly. "But I'm worried about Pamela. Where could she be?"

There was a confusion of voices, then someone said, "Try Michael's room. He might know."

Pamela froze, her hand to her mouth, while Michael chuckled.

The tour guide's voice answered firmly. "Mr. Donovan has just returned from a very tiring trip and he must get his rest. I refuse to disturb him at this point. Perhaps later, if the young woman still hasn't turned up."

"Good old Bob," Michael muttered. Pamela started to giggle and Michael held her close to his chest to hide the sound of it, chuckling himself. They heard evidence that the group retreating down the stairs, then both burst into laughter.

"Stay with me," he said again, his hand behind her head, fingers threading through her thick hair. "I'll tell them you're walking back to town."

She giggled again, a hysterical bubble rising in her throat. "Walking back to town! That would take hours."

"Of course." He grinned like a triumphant wolf. "That would be why you wouldn't arrive until tomorrow morning."

She laughed softly, luxuriously, loving him, and suddenly he'd reversed their positions on the bed, and she was looking up at his large body above hers.

"You're so beautiful," he said, his gaze still sparkling with amusement. "You know what those dark eyes remind me of right now?" He grinned. "Chocolate melting in the sun."

"Ooh." She grimaced. "Sounds messy."

"Messy," he agreed, leaning close to nip at the tip of her nose, "but delicious."

His mouth captured hers in a kiss that destroyed her defenses. "Hmm," he murmured, his breath mingling with hers, "my strength seems to be returning."

She smiled up at him, her eyes misty with longing. "You swore you were too tired to threaten me," she protested without much conviction.

"I lied," he replied shamelessly. He nibbled her earlobe. "My second wind has arrived," he said softly. "And it's bound to be a hurricane."

She flowered beneath his caresses, kissing him back with a fervor that would have astonished her if she'd been able to see herself. His hands explored her body, cupping her breast, stroking her flat stomach, pressing into the soft flesh of her back, bringing her to life in a way she'd only dreamed of.

It was a revelation, an awakening. Now she knew how it felt to be a woman. Now she knew what she'd been waiting for. She needed a man, and the man she needed was Michael. She loved him, wanted him—she would take him with the doubts if she couldn't have him any other way. She was ready. She knew she couldn't turn away again.

She put her hand on the smooth warmth of Michael's skin, touching the area around his navel, and suddenly a shudder ran through him, a tremor as strong as an earthquake jarring a mountain, and he wrenched away from her, flinging himself onto the far side of the bed.

"You'd better go, Pamela," he said hoarsely, his blue eyes narrowed as though he were in pain. "You'd better go while I can still let you."

"Michael..." She reached for him, not sure what she was doing, only knowing she would do anything to make him happy, but he caught her wrist and held it tightly.

"Go now, Pamela," he repeated evenly. "Go now, or you'll be staying for good."

She wanted to stay. Didn't he know that? But as her mind cleared, she knew he was right. She couldn't stay. She almost grinned as she imagined herself telling the group that she'd decided to spend the night with the man they'd come to pass judgment on.

"I'll go," she agreed, but she couldn't stop looking at him, her love in her eyes.

He reached out his hand for her hair spilling it through his fingers. "I've never waited so long for what I wanted before," he said musingly, more to himself than to her. "When will you come back to stay?"

Stay? As in "for the night"? He'd said "for good" a moment before, but what exactly had he meant? She searched his eyes, trying to read his full meaning. "Not until after the town meeting," she said. "I think I should stay away from you until then."

He nodded and she rose from the bed, adjusting her clothes and looking in his mirror to straighten her hair.

"But after the town meeting, we're going to put aside all these scruples," he said softly. "After the town meeting, you're coming with me."

She felt happiness surge through her. She would go with him, and stay as long as he wanted her. "Goodbye, Michael," she said quietly.

He didn't say anything. He just lay watching her, his eyes deep as mountain lakes.

She left his room and closed the door, leaning against it for a moment, gathering strength. "I'll miss you," she whispered, already filled with the ache of longing for him.

SHE RODE BACK to town with the other committee members. Her own car was parked at Mrs. Gimbel's house so she got out with the older woman and waved goodbye to the others. Then Mrs. Gimbel surprised her by asking, "Did you get a chance to speak to Michael Donovan?"

She'd told them only that she'd been exploring, and she hoped she didn't look guilty as she answered, "Yes, for a few minutes. Why?"

They were standing by Pamela's car. She could see Petrushka guarding the entryway of Mrs. Gimbel's lovely house, looking motherly and silly at the same time.

"Oh, I'm glad," Mrs. Gimbel replied. "He's the one who suggested you be asked to join the committee, you know."

"He is?" That was something of a shock. Why would he have done that? Pamela felt a cold shiver zigzag down her spine. She hated these suspicious thoughts. It seemed that whenever she thought she'd found explanations and excuses for them all, a new one came to the surface.

Here she was, crazy about the man, and every time she turned around there seemed to be a new reason she shouldn't be. Why couldn't it be easy? Why couldn't she just be free to love him and try to make him happy? Why did events and circumstances keep getting in the way?

But Mrs. Gimbel's smile showed she had no idea of Pamela's misgivings. "Yes, he particularly wanted to make sure you saw all the changes. He did so want to win you over."

"I see." Easy enough to win Pamela over, she thought with self-scorn. Just give her a tumble on the bed. Her face flamed with anger and some of it spilled into her voice as she replied. "I thought you were neutral."

"Oh, I am, dear." Mrs. Gimbel didn't take offense easily. "But I've known Michael's stepfather for years. I was the one who suggested Miracle Development look into White Acres when I first heard you might be selling."

Pamela stared at her. She hadn't known that. And yet, why not? She knew that Mrs. Gimbel and Mr. Harding had been friends for years. Mr. Harding had probably told her to be on the lookout for a buyer, as a favor to the Starbucks. What could be more natural? Who would have dreamed of the complexities that could arise from such a simple act?

The doubts nagged at her stubbornly, refusing to go away, no matter how she tried to suppress them. "That doesn't sound very neutral." She thought of Jeremy and his speeches about how men like Michael paved their way, how they bought off all the important people. Was he right?

Mrs. Gimbel smiled. "I didn't get a commission, if that's what you're thinking. But I am concerned with this town and have been trying for years to find ways to make it flourish. Believe me, if I see evidence that the development of White Acres is harmful to the valley, I'll be the first to condemn it." She patted Pamela's arm. "But I haven't seen that. In fact, quite the opposite. I think the resort is just what this community needs to lift us out of the doldrums we've been in for the past ten years or so. Fresh blood, new ideas—those things can't be harmful in moderation.''

Looking at the sincerity in her eyes, Pamela knew she was being honest about her own ethics. Mrs. Gimbel had the highest of reputations and she deserved it. She'd spent her life improving things in the valley. If she thought the development was going to be a plus, she was very likely right. So why did Pamela keep having these painful suspicions about everything connected with Michael? Was she letting her emotions cripple her critical thinking? She was ashamed.

''The resort seems to be very important to Michael,'' she said softly.

''Oh, yes,'' Mrs. Gimbel replied. ''Well, you know about his brothers, don't you?''

Pamela shook her head. She knew nothing about his family at all. In fact, she knew very little about him. All she knew was that she loved him.

''Stepbrothers, actually. Children of Marshall Bentworth's first wife. And that's the problem. They never quite accepted Michael, and when he turned out to be the one with a head for business like his stepfather's they always resented it. Now that Marshall has retired from taking an active part in the business, the three boys are jockeying for power, each trying to prove to their father that he's the one who's best.''

Proving things to fathers again. Just like Jeremy. So that was what Michael meant when he'd said he understood Jeremy better than she realized. They were two men trying to impress fathers. The best man would win and that had to be Michael. Jeremy was a nice kid with high ideals, but he was no match for Michael.

"The consensus," Mrs. Gimbel was saying, "is that Michael is the one who should run the company, but his brothers have precedence through blood relationship and age, so the burden of proof is on Michael. The success of this White Acres project will confirm his leadership. He'd do anything to make a go of it."

Her last words rang in Pamela's ears. He'd do anything...anything...anything. Did that include making her fall in love with him? Was it just part of his master plan? She hated to think that way, but there was always something forcing her to. After all, he'd lied to her from the first. Wasn't manipulating someone by withholding the truth a kind of a lie?

"Well, get along home, dear. I'm sure you're tired. We'll be getting together tomorrow to write up a report for the town meeting. Let's hope we can get things settled then."

Pamela spent a sleepless night. At three in the morning, when it became obvious she wasn't going to sleep at all, she went to her bureau drawer and pulled out the dried and faded gardenia garland Michael had made for her the night of Philip's party. She went back to sit on her bed and held it in her hand, gazing through her window at the moonlit forest, trying to sort out her feelings.

She was in love with Michael Donovan. That much she was sure of. The rest seemed to swirl around in her head like a winter storm. A few facts came to rest when she focused on them. He was fighting for control of his father's company. He'd lost a resort area once before, when local people objected. When he came to White Acres, he must have come fully prepared, knowing it could happen again, guarding against it. And he'd done his work well. He'd quickly turned influential people like Philip and Bernice to his side. The town had given him all the permits he needed without a protest. And then Jeremy had begun his battle.

But Michael had shown an interest in her long before Jeremy came on the scene, she reassured herself. And she knew it wasn't all to ensure his success, didn't she? He'd walked up the hill toward her and she'd watched him and something magical had happened. He'd mentioned it, too.

When they'd met again at Philip's party it had been as though no time had passed. They'd come together like two parts of a whole, fitting like pieces of a jigsaw puzzle. She'd felt as though it was meant to be. And then she'd discovered he hadn't come back to search her out at all. He was there to promote his resort project. If she hadn't been at the party, would he have come looking for her? And if he had, would he have come because he couldn't stay away, or because he wanted her on his side?

On the one hand her natural wariness persisted; on the other, she hated herself for being so suspicious of the man she loved. Closing her eyes, she wished the town meeting was over already. It was two days away. Two days, and then the truth would settle.

CHAPTER TEN

THE TWO DAYS seemed to drag by. The shop was just about ready for a grand opening. She was quite pleased with her displays, glowing with pride, when one visitor remarked, "You'd make a good museum curator." Yet that wasn't her job. She was supposed to be selling things. But, sales had been sparse, although she did sell two more Russian ducks to ladies who'd seen Mrs. Gimbel's.

"Suzy?" she said musingly as she gazed at the two remaining ducks. They looked so lonely without the others. "Do we have that woman's address?"

"What woman?" Suzy asked distractedly. Jeremy's crusade was beginning to wear on her, and she had dark circles under her eyes. Everytime she went out, people stopped her to ask her opinion on the White Acres matter. And they also asked her Pamela's. For some reason they didn't seem to want to approach her sister directly. But Suzy didn't know what her own opinion was, much less Pam's. She loved White Acres, but she was young and ready to move on to other things. If Jeremy hadn't started his crusade she was sure she would have lived quite happily with the new resort. As it was, she had to back Jeremy. But she did not do so very enthusiastically.

"The woman with the ducks," Pamela answered. "Do you suppose we could order more?"

A sly grin appeared on Suzy's pretty face. "What?" she said as though thunder struck. "More ducks? Do you really think the Indians would approve?"

Pamela made a face at her. "The Indians love the ducks, and so do I. Let's order six more."

At that moment Mr. Scofield entered the shop. "These ducks are going fast," he commented. "I want to buy one before they're all gone. Want to give it to my daughter for her new house down in Hanford."

Pamela glanced at them wistfully. "Do you want to take it now?" she asked sadly.

He put his money on the counter. "Might as well. Going out to see my daughter on the weekend. And I think my wife would like to have that little fat waddler around for a few days before we go." He scratched his chin and looked at the remaining two. "I wonder if Hildie wouldn't like one, too. . ." he began.

"Oh, I'm sorry. The last one is reserved," Pamela said quickly, ignoring Suzy's derisive snicker in the background. "We'll be ordering more, though," she added apologetically. "I don't know when they'll come in."

"We ought to give up on this other stuff and go into the duck business," Suzy commented after Mr. Scofield left. "They're going like hotcakes."

But Suzy had bad news for her a little later that day. "I guess I didn't get an address, after all," she said after she'd spent some time searching. "Without an address, how can we order any more of them?"

Pamela knew it was silly to consider no more ducks such a tragedy, but somehow it was. She took in the last duck and set it on the shop counter, even though it was too big and looked out of place there. She wasn't going to take any chances with her only remaining duck.

"Anna Karenina," she said under her breath, looking at the silly animal. "That's your name." She could have sworn the duck smiled just a little.

The committee held its meeting and every member had to admit that Michael's company had done a good job. One man was still concerned about the increase in traffic and another hated any sort of change on the river—no matter what it was—but they couldn't cite Michael for anything specific. They agreed to abide by a report Mrs. Gimbel had written with one dissenting amendment.

Unless Jeremy could come up with some surprise ammunition, Pamela didn't see how he could win this one. However, he seemed in good spirits before the town meeting. When he came to get Suzy he was raring to go, paying hardly any attention to Pamela's complaints about her photograph being used without her permission.

"I didn't claim you were backing me," he protested cheerfully. "I was just filling in the history of the place. You can't argue with that."

Pamela was so sure he was going to lose his bid, that she didn't have the heart to stay angry with him. "Just don't do it again," she said weakly and left it at that.

But Jeremy was full of excitement. "We've got old Donovan on the run," he insisted. "Have you heard? He's got labor problems. There are pickets at the entrance to his construction site, and they're hopping mad. Even his employees are turning against him. Believe me, Pamela, we're going to stop that resort yet."

"I'm not part of the 'we,'" she retorted, but he didn't listen. No one ever listened, she realized. Everyone assumed she was against the development of White Acres. Why didn't anyone ever ask her directly?

What was the answer? She knew she hadn't really enjoyed seeing the changes Michael had made. Would she be more upset about them if she hadn't fallen in love with him? Would she be helping Jeremy? She wasn't sure.

She rode to the meeting with Jeremy and Suzy, and as Jeremy helped her out of the car, she saw Michael watching from across the street. She started to wave, but he turned away and she saw the red pamphlet in his hand.

She stood on the sidewalk, stunned. She'd known he wouldn't like seeing her picture used that way, but it had never occurred to her that he might be so angry that he wouldn't even give her a chance to explain. Maybe he was just preoccupied. He was about to participate in a meeting that might decide some very important issues in his life. He was bound to be caught up in the tension. She would have to wait until later to confront him and find out what he really thought.

The meeting hall was packed with people, and the buzz of their conversation was dizzying. She made her way through the crowd until she found a place to sit near the front, Suzy and Jeremy beside her. Glancing to the right, she saw Michael enter and sit across the hall. He didn't look in her direction.

The mayor called the meeting to order, and gradually the noise died down. The mayor set forth the problem, giving a bit of the background, and all the while, Pamela could see Jeremy fidgeting next to Suzy. He was nervous and he was excited, twisting around every few minutes to peer into the back of the hall. She knew he thought he had a good case, but she suspected Michael would have a better one, so she felt sorry for him. He was a good kid, just a little intense.

Suddenly he seemed to find what he was looking for at the back of the room. A huge smile lit his narrow face. "We've got it made," he whispered loudly, grinning at everyone who turned to see what he was talking about. "This one's in the bag." He craned his neck to look at Michael. "Squirm, Donovan," he muttered.

The mayor chose that moment to call Jeremy forward to present his case. He took the microphone and began reciting the now-familiar litany of reasons the White Acres development would be ruinous to their valley. "Rural area...river pollution...overloaded sewage systems...insufficient access roads...traffic congestion...crime...tourists..." But Pamela wasn't really listening. She was watching Michael out of the corner of her eye. He looked serenely confident. Every now and then he leaned over to Bob, the assistant who'd been their tour guide the other day, and said something that caused his friend to laugh. He looked every inch a winner. Did poor Jeremy stand a chance?

"I know you've all heard me say my piece before," Jeremy was saying. "And I've shown you slides and film presentations to prove my point." He grinned impishly. "And some of you got my point. But some of you still aren't sure. So I tried to think what I could do to convince the nonbelievers." He grinned again. "And I came upon a little information that just might do the trick. You see, our friend Michael Donovan—" he gestured toward where Michael was sitting "—has tried this sort of thing before. There's a little town in Oregon that once went through just what we're going through now. And they came to their senses and booted Miracle Development out before things went too far. I've brought a couple of people from that little town here tonight to tell you their story in their own words.''

The two people Jeremy referred to were walking up to the podium, but Pamela wasn't looking at them. She was staring at Michael, stabbed by the accusation in his eyes as he stared back.

He thought she'd given Jeremy that information. He'd told her about it while she was in his room rubbing his back, and he thought she'd run off and told Jeremy to search for a town in Oregon named Yellowfin where he could get information on Michael's previous failure. Well, she hadn't! It had never even occurred to her to tell him. Jeremy must have found out from his contacts in Berkeley. But how could she make Michael believe that?

The two men from Oregon told a tale that hinted at underhand dealings and illicit motives and concluded with the good townsfolk casting out the evil developers. By the time they'd finished there was a hum of whispering in the hall. They'd made points people couldn't ignore. Maybe there was more to this Miracle Development company than met the eye. Maybe they ought to rethink just a little. After all, here was a town just like theirs....

When Michael finally got up to speak, the air of distrust was palpable. The people who had once been so friendly were breathing hostility. They weren't sure whom to believe, and they were ready to lash out at Michael. Pamela ached to protect him. She had an irrational urge to run to the front of the auditorium and scream at them all. Her hands were clammy, and her heart was beating very fast. Regardless of anything else, he was her man, and she was ready to do whatever it took to help him.

Michael stood in front of the crowd for a long moment, his gaze sweeping from one end of the hall to the other. He looked into Pamela's eyes, but his own were blank and emotionless. He obviously felt the townspeople's antagonism and regretted it, but it was equally obvious that he felt he could deal with it. Suddenly he smiled, and in that one simple gesture, Pamela could sense the room begin to relax.

Then he spoke. He didn't say anything substantial at first, just rambled, talking gently about the valley and how much he liked it, the people he'd met, the things he'd seen. He mentioned Jerry Renault and his candles, Sheree Craighton and her lovely jewelry and some of the other local people with whom he'd come in contact since he'd arrived. Smiles began to appear again. He took up one point the Oregonians had made, then another, not refuting accusations as much as ridiculing them in the gentlest of ways. Little by little his superb persuasion was bringing his listeners around.

When he raised the subject of employment and mentioned a job he had given to Sheree Craighton's crippled husband, he had his audience in the palm of his hand. He played them like a fine instrument, knowing just how to pluck the strings to get the tone he wanted. He was a master, and Pamela was stunned at his power.

A moment before, she'd been aching for Michael and now her heart went out to Jeremy. Michael was winning, and it really wasn't fair. Not that she wanted him to lose. But he was winning on charm and personality, while Jeremy had tried to win on facts—at least, what he thought were facts. The people liked Michael, instinctively trusted him. She could feel the trust grow as he spoke. They were ready to hand over the reins to Michael Donovan. He could lead them wherever he thought it best.

He finished, to a loud round of applause, and returned to his seat. Mrs. Gimbel then read the committee's favorable report. The mayor took a vote, and Michael won by an overwhelming majority. There would be no further roadblocks to the success of the White Acres resort.

Pamela glanced at Jeremy. While Michael had seemed to grow in stature as he stood before the crowd, Jeremy had shrunk. He looked old and shriveled sitting beside Suzy, as though all his fight had been drained away. His face was ashen and he seemed stunned, confused, as though he wasn't sure just how Michael had outwitted him. Suzy looked pale, too, and when Jeremy suddenly lurched to his feet, stumbling by Pamela toward the exit, Suzy followed him.

Pamela stood, uncertain what she should do. She belonged with Michael. That was what he'd said at White Acres two days earlier. They'd both agreed that was the way it would be once the meeting was over. In her heart, she exulted with him in his victory. But he was riding so high right now. The people crowded around him as though he'd just won a presidential election, everyone wanting to get in a word, shake his hand. Jeremy was being ignored, and Jeremy was the one in pain. She was torn, not sure which way to move.

Suzy pushed her way back through the crowd. "Pamela!" she called. "Please come! Jeremy's acting crazy. I'm afraid he's going to do something...."

She started to follow her sister, and suddenly Michael was standing before her. His blue eyes burned, but there was no warmth in his gaze as he looked into hers. Still he wanted her. "The town meeting is over, Pamela," he said evenly. "Are you coming with me?"

She stopped, hand to her throat. She'd promised, hadn't she? And she wanted to got with him. It was where she belonged. And yet here was Suzy calling, "Please, Pamela! Hurry. I can't handle him by myself." She looked at her sister, and knew she couldn't refuse the pleading in Suzy's eyes.

"I—I can't," she said to Michael, reaching for him, wanting a moment to explain. "I've got to—"

He evaded her touch. "Don't try to explain, Pamela," he said bitingly. "I think I get the picture." He turned his back on her and was immediately swallowed by the crowd of happy well-wishers. Anguish shivered through her and she turned to Bob, who was still standing beside her.

"Tell him I'll call him," she said in a rush. "I've got to help Suzy with Jeremy, but I'll call him as soon—"

"Why don't you just give up?" Bob said scornfully. "The resort's going to be built. You can't do any more to stop it."

She gaped at him, surprised. "No, you don't understand—"

"I understand," he said. "We both know what you've been up to. You've been trying to weasel information out of Michael for weeks. He set up that whole committee visit in order to get you out to White Acres to see what he was doing, just to ease your mind, and you used the opportunity to search his room for evidence against him."

"What?" Pamela gasped, too shocked to defend herself.

"We know how you operate, lady. And Michael may go for you in a big way, but business comes first. It always has, and it always will." His smile was openly malicious. He wiggled his eyebrows at her and walked away.

Pamela moved in a cloud of unreality. As she followed Suzy to the bar, where Jeremy had retreated to down several drinks in quick succession, and helped her force him out of the smoke-filled room and into the car, she hardly knew what she was doing. It couldn't be true, could it? Michael couldn't really believe that of her. He couldn't possible think she'd only been pretending to love him in order to gain information to use against him—and that she'd gone into his room to search. If he did, why had he acted so happy to see her there? Or had it only been later that he'd come to that conclusion? Later, after he'd seen the pamphlets and watched as Jeremy brought in the Oregonians.

She had to call him. She had to make him listen. She loved him. Didn't he know that?

But Jeremy's pain demanded all her energy for the next few hours, and when she and Suzy finally got him to sleep on their sofa, it was well after midnight.

"Tomorrow," she murmured to herself. "I'll go to him first thing in the morning and make him understand."

She slept fitfully, tossing and turning. She dreamed of Michael and he was angry. When she awoke, with a start her eyes stung with unshed tears. Suddenly she realized that the telephone was ringing.

"Oh, Pamela!" Bernice's voice was high with concern. "Where is Jeremy? Have you seen him?"

"Yes, he's right—" she craned her neck around the corner to make sure of her facts and saw Jeremy's tousled head "—here on our couch. What's the matter?"

Bernice breathed a sigh of relief. "Someone burned down White Acres during the night and the police seem to think Jeremy did it. Was he with you all night?"

"Michael?" she whispered hoarsely. "Is he...?"

"I don't know a thing about it," Bernice snapped. "But what about Jeremy? Was he with you all night?"

Pamela went cold and couldn't answer. Suzy had come out of her room and was asking "Who is it?" Pamela handed the receiver to her without a word and stumbled to her bedroom, reaching for her clothes. White Acres, burned. She couldn't think about it. She had to go out and see for herself. Throat aching and hands trembling, she pulled on slacks and a sweater and rummaged for her car keys.

"Where are you going?" Suzy cried wildly.

"You stay here," she said in a monotone. "The police will probably be here soon, and you'll have to vouch for the fact that Jeremy was here all night." She looked at Suzy sharply. "He was, wasn't he?"

Suzy shrugged helplessly. "I think so," she whispered.

But Pamela didn't want to think about it at all. She just wanted to see if Michael was safe. And what had happened to White Acres.

CHAPTER ELEVEN

THERE WAS NO SMOKE hanging over White Acres as she drove in through the high white gate. In fact, the morning was glorious, without a cloud in the sky. But she could smell the acrid evidence of what had happened during the night. As she rounded the bend and started up the hill, she sagged with relief when she saw the main house still standing. That meant Michael should be all right. Unless he'd done something crazy, like fighting the fires by himself.

Tears filled her eyes, and she angrily blinked them back so that she could see just what the extent of the damage was. Pulling the car to a stop, she jumped out and looked around. Three of the cottages were totally destroyed, with only their brick fireplaces left standing, and two were gutted but the walls were still in place. The surrounding trees were singed. Some looked like spent torches.

Except for the trees, the only damage seemed to be to structures Michael had put up. Pamela stood and stared at the burnt relics, swallowing hard. Why did she feel so devastated? The house, her house, had been spared. And yet, she felt as though she, too, had been violated.

"Not a pretty sight, is it?"

Michael's voice was anything but welcoming, but when she spun around and saw him standing there, she couldn't restrain herself. She flew into his arms, tears spilling down her cheeks. "Oh, Michael! Thank God you're all right!"

He held her for a moment. "Yes, I'm all right," he said gruffly, though he didn't try to keep her from drawing away. "And the fire didn't reach the house." He narrowed his eyes, looking at the cinders. "But then, I don't suppose that was the plan."

"The plan?" she asked innocently. "What do you mean? What plan?"

His blue gaze was knife sharp as it cut through her. "I think you know that as well as anyone, Pamela."

Surely he wasn't accusing her! But she seemed to be defending herself against all sorts of things lately. Why not this too? "No, I don't think I do," she said coldly. "Perhaps you'd better explain it to me."

He shrugged. He was wearing a heavy fisherman's sweater and faded jeans and he looked more handsome than she'd ever seen him. But less attractive, somehow. Colder. Humorless. "The fire department found clear evidence of arson. You friend Jeremy Keaton lost out in the town meeting," he said casually, as though it was something any fool could see, "so he tried to win by torching my resort. What could be simpler?"

Pamela's eyes flashed. "It's simple all right," she snapped. "Simpleminded thinking. Jeremy did no such thing."

He turned on her, fury boiling over. "You're still going to defend him after this?" he snarled, his arm sweeping wide to encompass the destruction. "The man's a maniac, and if the police don't take care of him, I will."

She stared at him in horror, visions of what he might do to Jeremy whirling through her head. "Jeremy didn't do this. You've got to believe me. He was on our couch all night. He couldn't have done it."

Michael's face turned to stone. "Are you telling me you're going to give him his alibi?" he asked, his voice razor edged.

She was shivering but she managed to lift her chin high. "It's only the truth, Michael. He was so upset last night he tried to drink himself into a stupor. We dragged him home and filled him with coffee and put him on the couch. He was still there when Bernice called me this morning and told me about the fire."

Michael didn't bend. "He did it, Pamela. And if you're covering for him, you're either a fool or a liar."

His words cut deep but she struggled against the pain. "He didn't do it," she insisted, swallowing tears.

He shook his head as though he couldn't understand her position. "Who else would have done it?" he asked. "Who else had his motive?"

She turned away. "I don't know. I only know it wasn't Jeremy."

She could feel the rage in him without having to look at his face to see it. Suddenly he seized her arm, and began to pull her toward the main house, "Come here. I want to show you something." She ran beside him as fast as she could, finding it almost impossible to keep pace with his long stride. He led her around the house to the back corner. The fire had come much closer than she'd thought. Her favorite childhood hiding place had been in the bramble bushes outside the back door. Half of them were gone now, singed and black.

"He didn't do such a good job, did he?" Michael asked sarcastically. "That's how close it came. If I hadn't been up, unable to sleep, it would have taken the house before anyone saw it. Your house. Now what do you think of your good friend Jeremy Keaton?"

She stared at the withered bushes and tried to speak, but there were no words. It had come so close. Another few minutes and the house would have been destroyed. Michael had saved it for her. But Michael was the reason the fire had been started in the first place. At least, he seemed to be. If Jeremy hadn't done it, and she didn't think he had, who then? And why? Her head was spinning in confusion and Michael's next move didn't help.

He grasped her shoulders in his large hands and forced her to look up into his face, pinning her with his ice-blue gaze. "You're going to have to decide where you stand, Pamela," he said hoarsely. "You can't wander back and forth across the battle lines."

She blinked up at him. "I'm not," she tried to say, but the words didn't sound right, even to her.

"I know it upset you when you had to sell your land. And then to find out I was going to develop it— you resented that. I can understand. And I tried to give you space to come to grips with it on your own. But the time has come to choose sides. I want you to choose, and I want you to choose right now. I can't wait any longer."

She shook her head, trying to clear it, and he took her action for denial.

"Yes, dammit," he growled, his hands moving up to capture her face. "Choose now, Pamela."

She gasped as his mouth came down to smother hers. His kiss was hot with passion, hard with anger, and she tried to pull loose. But he was not prepared to tolerate evasion. He was set to master her as he'd mastered the crowd the night before.

Belatedly he seemed to remember that he'd won with persuasion and charm rather than by bludgeoning, and his kiss began to soften accordingly. What had initially been raw and forceful quickly became a coaxing caress, and instead of trying to push him away, she found herself melting into his arms.

She moaned softly as he turned to sweet seduction. She couldn't resist his tenderness. His kiss grew warmer, deeper, and his embraces began to suffuse her body with a tingle that would lead to her surrender in no time at all. She found herself reaching for more, kissing him back, digging her fingers into the thick thatch of his hair, pressing the soft curves of her body against the hard angles of his.

"Pamela, Pamela," he breathed into her flowing hair. "You belong here with me. Say you'll stay. I need you in my bed tonight."

And how she wanted to be there! But she couldn't say yes. Not yet. Not while this mess was still hanging over their heads.

A day or so ago she'd thought everything would be settled by whatever happened at the town meeting. She hadn't foreseen that the meeting would be not the end of a problem but the beginning of one. There was no turning back at this point, no way of pretending that things between them were simple and clear. She had to play out the hand she'd been dealt. If she could only think clearly, she might be able to give him some sort of promise for the future. But he wanted more.

"Choose now," he was demanding. "I need to know now."

She pulled out of his arms and began walking blindly away from him, toward the front of the house.

"Where are you going?" he called after her, though he didn't make a move to follow.

"I don't know," she whispered, holding back the tears that were so close to the surface.

"If you leave now," he said, his voice as final as a death verdict, "I'll consider that your answer."

She turned to look back at him, but his image swam in the moisture that filled her eyes. "I have to go," she whispered just loudly enough for him to hear. "I have to think."

He didn't say a word and she turned and ran toward her car. Jumping in, she switched on the engine and roared down the drive, not daring to see if he was following. She had to get away, away from Michael, away from the valley, away from everything. She had to find a place to hide, a place where she could think and make a rational decision. She headed north, for the high, cool mountains of Yosemite.

The sky had been clear down in the foothills, but as she climbed into the mountains, clouds began to form around the peaks.

"You got chains with you?" the ranger at the entrance to the park asked. "We might be getting a little powder before nightfall."

She did have chains in the trunk of her car and sure enough, as she drove through some of the highest passes, there were a few brief snow flurries. But by the time she reached the bottom of Yosemite Valley, the sun was out again. Nevertheless, it was cold.

She was lucky to get a room at the lodge. Yosemite was always full, but there was a cancellation and she quickly took the room, even though it was a double and bordered the shops. It seemed odd to check into a room without baggage. She went shopping right away and used her credit card to acquire a down jacket for the cold and some toilet articles for the night. She spent too much money but didn't let herself worry about it. This was survival.

She found warm gloves in the car, put on her new down jacket and began walking. She walked and walked and walked, until she felt as though she'd covered half the park. The shuttle bus passed her every now and then, and people waved, but she had no impulse to join them. She'd come here because she wanted to be alone. When she found the right place, she would stop and think. And then it would all become clear.

Did she really believe that? Probably not. But if she couldn't hope for understanding, what could she hope for?

So she kept walking. As the shadows grew longer, she began to see deer. The does came out of the woods cautiously, looking about for danger, then stalking purposefully toward a likely bush. They didn't seem afraid of her as she passed, but continued to chew and stare with huge, sad eyes as though they wondered why she wasn't eating, too.

Wandering through a redwood grove, she felt, as she always did, a deep sense of reverence. The huge, beautiful trees seemed to form a natural cathedral. It humbled her just to walk among them.

Redwood trees. Jeremy had told her about a campaign he'd been involved in to save the redwood trees in a county up north. It seemed that everything needed saving these days. So many kinds of life in trouble, so many species becoming extinct—all except mankind. The human species seemed remarkably resilient.

Why was that, she wondered, then answered her own question. Adaptability, of course. Mankind could change when circumstances warranted adjustments.

She stopped dead in her tracks. How adaptable was she? How easily had she accepted change when it was inevitable? Perhaps that was part of her problem, an inability to bend. She knew that those who didn't bend risked breaking. Had she fallen into that trap without realizing it?

She thought she'd done so well, accepted things so bravely. But had she really? Or had her apparent acceptance disguised her real feelings, even from herself?

She'd been sickened at seeing her land charred and blackened. Somehow that had finally brought it home to her—the fact that the land was no longer hers, that it would never be the same as it once had been. Had she really come to terms with Michael's being in charge, with Michael's making so many changes? Had she really let herself deal with it fully? Perhaps not. Perhaps she should.

Michael had continually treated her as someone who needed to be convinced. The enemy. Just the way she'd treated him. Even so, she'd resented it. But maybe he was right. Not that she would spy for Jeremy, but that she wasn't ready to accept Michael wholeheartedly, to let him be what he was.

She puzzled over her new perspective as she walked slowly back to the lodge. Some of the questions were clearer, but she still didn't have the answers.

When she got back she called Suzy and told her she was all right but not to expect her back for a day or two. She wouldn't tell her sister where she was and hung up quickly, not waiting for a long discourse on what had happened since she'd left. She didn't want to give Suzy time to pick up any clues about where she was staying. She was sure no one would think of looking at Yosemite. They would expect her to run to San Francisco or Fresno—or maybe Sacramento where she still had friends. But never to Yosemite. Only tourists went there.

Smart tourists, she thought as she gazed out at the magnificent scenery. There was such peacefulness here in the valley, such a serenity of spirit. Human affairs came and went, but the mountains and rivers never changed.

All right, they did change. She'd studied geology in school, and she knew that as well as anyone. But it took millions of years and she thought she could be allowed a little poetic license.

She went to the restaurant and ate alone, watching the happy family groups and the young couples. The park wasn't nearly as full as it was in the summer when the cabins and tents were available, too, but there were plenty of people about. Everyone loved Yosemite. Who could help it?

On her way back from the restaurant she stopped at the market to buy something to drink. Her hand hovered over a bottle of wine, but when she came right down to it, it wasn't really what she wanted. She picked up a jug of orange soda instead and went to her room and drank it from a water glass—once again, all alone. The distant sounds of music and dancing at the visitor's center jangled through the night, reinforcing her loneliness. She turned on one small lamp against the darkness and sat at the little round table, leaving the drapes open so she could see the mountains. And she tried to break through the feelings to catch hold of the truths below.

She had with her the little bag of gold nuggets Michael had given her. She shook it empty, spilling them onto the table. They looked like teardrops in the dim light. Tears of gold. Tears from her land.

And then it was as though the floodgates opened at last. She began to cry for her land and for her father and mother and all her family who'd possessed the land and lived and died there. She cried for Suzy and Jeremy and Michael and the burned cottages—and for herself. She cried aloud, letting the tears flow without any shame or inhibition, cried as she'd never cried before, not even that morning when she'd signed the papers to give up White Acres. All the rage and pain that had been hidden inside cascaded from her in great waves of grief.

It lasted a long time, but when she was finished, she felt calmer, almost relieved, as though something fundamental had changed in her life. She put the gold nuggets away and fell dreamlessly asleep. She was up early in the morning, walking to Bridalveil Fall and back before breakfast.

The hike gave her a big appetite and she ate with greedy pleasure—eggs and bacon and pancakes and juice, as well as her usual coffee. She didn't know why she was feeling so cheerful. Nothing had been resolved. No answers had come to her in the night. But she felt like smiling at everyone she met and she made another hike, this time to Mirror Lake and back. Then she ate another big meal for lunch and went out to explore the shops and galleries.

As she was walking back to the lodge, taking a shortcut through the residential area used by people who worked in the valley, a flash of something familiar caught her eye. She stopped to look. There on a small front porch sat a sister to Olga and Petrushka and her own Anna. Another duck with a babushka on its silly head.

Without a second thought she walked quickly to the door, giving the orange bill a friendly stroke as she went by. A pretty young woman answered, smiling at her questioningly.

"Where did you get the duck?" Pamela asked without preamble.

The young woman laughed. "Everyone asks that," she said. "Isn't she a doll? My aunt makes them. She lives in Fish Camp. If you're planning to go through there on your way home..."

Pamela was planning just that, and she got the address of the aunt. As she returned to her room, she felt as exultant as if she'd just found a gold mine.

And in a way she had. After all, the ducks had begun to be about the most successful item she carried. With a bit of promotion they might really take off. And if the woman was so good at ducks, what else might she have up her sleeve?

Pamela laughed at herself. Dopey over ducks. Who would have thought she'd get this way when she'd made her big plans for her shop? Wasn't that always the way, though? A person might plan and scheme and nothing works out, then something that was hardly noticed comes in and saves the day.

She stopped to watch the water raging over the rocks of a riverbed and thought about the paradoxes of her life. Was it all that way? Had she spent too much time worrying about what she considered the big issues and let the really important things slip through her fingers? If she thought back over the past few months and singled out the best thing that had happened in her life, she'd have to admit it was falling in love with Michael.

That was it. She'd found the man of her dreams. Did she want him or not? What did it matter that in the beginning he'd kept from her his real reasons for being at White Acres? Would she still have loved him if he'd told her? Of course. Would he still have been attracted to her if she'd been just a guest at that first party instead of the hostess and owner of White Acres? She had no doubt about it.

Then what had all this turmoil been for? Why did she spend her time wondering why he'd said this and why he hadn't said that, what he really meant and what he thought she'd done? None of it mattered.

For so long she hadn't allowed herself to trust him, and then she'd found out there were reasons he might not trust her. It had all been a ridiculous red herring, anyway. She'd tortured herself with questions about Michael, and all the while the only real problem had been that she hadn't come to terms with her sorrows and losses of the past few years. There had been so much pain that she hadn't worked through it yet.

But now she had. With quiet satisfaction, she realized the truth. It was over. It was time to deal with important things.

Michael was the man she loved. If she wanted him, she was going to have to go out and get him. It was time to take charge of her life, to fight for what she wanted.

Picking up a rounded stone, she threw it as far down the river as she could, then she turned and started to run back to her room. She wasn't happy. In fact, she was very, very frightened. But she knew where she wanted to go now. And she was determined to get there.

It took only a few minutes to check out of her room and toss her things into the car. Then she was off, heading back home. Heading for Michael. And so frightened of what she would find when she got to him.

CHAPTER TWELVE

THE AFTERNOON SUN was hanging like an orange
pumpkin in the sky when she arrived at White Acres.
Unlike the day before, there were cloud banks ringing
the valley. Evidence of a coming storm? she asked
herself, biting her lip. She hoped not.

Her thoughts turned to Michael. The day before
when she'd run from him, he'd told her to choose. "If
you leave," he'd said, "I'll consider that your answer." When Michael said something like that, he
meant it. She'd seen him in action often enough to
know. Would it be too late to go to him now? Would
he accept her or send her away? She'd never been so
worried before. Nothing had ever been so important
before.

She drove up near the house, parking in front of one
of the temporary trailers that housed the administra-
tion. She locked the car. The back seat was full of new
ducks. She'd stopped in Fish Camp and picked up as
many as she could carry.

The day before, the place had been deserted, but
today workmen's cars seemed to be everywhere. They
were already tearing down the burned structures and
putting up new wood frames. Michael worked fast.
Out with the old. In with the new. Pamela shivered as
she got out of the car.

Walking quickly, hoping she wasn't too late, she went into the trailer with the sign Personnel on it. There was a man behind a small desk and a row of chairs along one side. The man looked up with an impersonal smile as she entered.

"May I help you?" he asked in a monotone that said he'd repeated the same phrase in exactly the same way a few hundred times.

"I understand you're taking applications for the resort," she said, clenching her hands to force herself to stand there and not bolt for the door.

"That's right." He nodded. "We plan to open in March, but we'll need a full staff before then to help get ready. What sort of employment are you interested in?"

She hesitated. When she'd had the idea of using this as a way of showing Michael how she felt, it had seemed so simple. She'd imagined herself walking in and offering her services while Michael beamed in the background, only to rush forward immediately and sweep her into his arms almost before she had a chance to get the words out. It obviously wasn't going to work that way. Michael didn't seem to be around, and she couldn't ask this man to please wait with his questions until the boss could serve as audience. He'd think she was crazy.

"I guess I'd be most interested in running the gift shop," she said as inspiration hit her. "I run a shop in town right now."

"Mmm." He frowned, looking at her. What if he already had that position filled? What if he sent her away? She could just see herself calling, "No wait, I'll take a waitress job if that's all you've got. I'll wash dishes!" while the man firmly shoved her out the door. Images of a dignified reconciliation were fading fast. "I guess I'd have to check with Mr. Donovan as to what his plans are there," he said slowly. "He's never asked me to find someone for the gift shop. I'd assumed he planned to bring in a manager from one of his other resorts." Then his face cleared. "But it wouldn't hurt to let you fill out an application."

She watched as he pulled out forms and pencils. "Here you go. We need three copies of this one. And four references, please. Oh, use the back of this one to describe the shop you have now. And why don't you include a little information about what you plan to do with it if and when you come to work for us?" He handed her a stack that looked like work enough for a week. "You can take any seat you like." Then his expression became remote again. As far as he was concerned he was finished with her for the day.

She stared at the papers, appalled. Did she really want to spend the rest of the afternoon filling out forms just to get an appointment with Michael? Surely there must be a better way. She closed her eyes briefly, steeling herself. She'd decided to fight for him, and she'd decided this was the way to start. She wasn't going to let a little paperwork deter her now.

"Will Mr. Donovan ever see this application?" she asked the personnel man.

He looked up as though surprised to see her still there. "Oh, yes. I screen them first, of course, and attach my recommendations. But Mr. Donovan insists on reviewing all of them himself." He smiled. "And if he feels you might have a chance with us, there would be an interview with Mr. Donovan. He makes all the final decisions."

Good. She smiled back and sat down to make her application for employment at White Acres Resort.

She filled in her name and address and previous employment record, her college experience and scholastic honors. She swore that she had never been convicted by a general court-martial, that she'd never been indicted on felony charges, that she didn't use controlled substances. Then came the hard part—a paragraph explaining why she wanted to work at White Acres.

She chewed on her eraser for a moment, then wrote a quick note on her experience, her love for the White Acres land, and ended with, "Finally and foremost, I want to work at White Acres Resort because I would be working for Michael Donovan. Mr. Donovan has already proved himself a success in the resort business, and he's about to crown his other achievements here. I'd like to be part of his triumph. He's the most wonderful man I've ever met, and I think I'm in love with him."

Her heart was beating very fast as she finished her paragraph. Was this ridiculous? Was she making a fool of herself? Probably. But her alternative was to walk in on him cold and begin apologizing—and then to say how she felt about him to his face. Somehow this seemed safer.

"Here you are," she said as she handed her papers in.

The man glanced at them, then at his watch. "If you like, I'll go over them right now," he said genially. "It's almost quitting time and I've got nothing more important to do."

She sat down in front of him, sliding to the edge of her chair, trying to create a picture of calm dignity.

And failing miserably. She watched his face as he read over her entries. At first he looked pleased, then impressed. Finally he got to her last paragraph, and suddenly his face went very blank. He stared at it for a long time, and she had the distinct impression he was dying to look at her but didn't dare to until he was totally composed.

"Well, well," he said, coughed, then coughed again. "I'll, uh, have to go into the other room to make a call."

He disappeared through a door and when she looked again, she saw him peering out at her. His face quickly vanished but a moment later he was back, a puzzled frown creasing his forehead.

"I'm just going to send these papers over..." he mumbled, calling in a young man and handing them to him. He glanced at Pamela, then looked fixedly at his desk, but he didn't tell her to leave. She stayed where she was and he shuffled and sorted his papers.

It was only a few minutes later that the telephone on his desk rang. He picked up the receiver and answered in monosyllables, finally putting it down and staring at his desk again. "As it happens," he said to Pamela, "Mr. Donovan is free right now. He's asked me to send you over to the main house. That is, if you're not in a hurry to get away."

She smiled at him graciously. "I have all the time in the world," she said with false calm. "Where will I find him?"

"In the...in the den," he said. He looked at her quickly, then down at his desk again. "Right away, he said." The poor man was evidently bewildered by what was going on and by his role as unwitting go-between.

"Thank you," she told him sincerely. She tripped down the stairs of the trailer and walked slowly toward the house. This was it. She had no idea how Michael would receive her. He might still consider her the enemy, the friend of an arsonist, the spy in his bedroom. Her heart was beating so hard she felt lightheaded and dizzy.

The front door was standing open. There was no one about so she walked in, heading straight for the den where her father had always done his work. That door was open, too, but only a crack. She knocked.

"Come in." She'd been expecting to hear Michael's voice but not quite so loud, and she jumped when he spoke. Taking a deep breath to steady herself, she entered.

He was sitting at the same desk where her father had once sat, only now it was piled high with papers. When her father had used it, there was usually nothing there but a racing form. He didn't look up as she entered. He had her application in his hands and seemed to be studying it intently. As she came near, he motioned for her to be seated, just as though she was an ordinary applicant.

"Briggs College," he murmured as he read. "Nice school."

"Yes, it was." She cursed herself for the tremor in her voice, then wished she hadn't spoken at all. Why should he care how nice her college was? It would be best to keep still and let him do the talking until she knew where she stood.

But what was happening here, anyway? She'd used the ploy of applying for a job to show him she was sincere and to get a chance to talk to him in a straightforward, unemotional way. She hadn't meant to carry the hoax any further. What was he doing?

"Honor society, Shutterbug club, an essay award, intercollegiate golf team..." He looked up for the first time but it was with the gaze of a stranger. He might never have seen her before in his life. "We have an opening for an assistant pro on the golf course. You wouldn't be interested in that?"

She shook her head, searching his eyes. She couldn't detect a flicker of humor anywhere. It was on the tip of her tongue to say, "Wait a minute, Michael, what are you doing?" But she saw the look in his eyes and decided that might not be prudent. He went on.

"Debating society, yearbook editor, calligraphy club. Never a cheerleader?"

"I was never the bouncy type," she said, a little startled. How long was he going to play this game?

"No," he replied thoughtfully, looking her up and down dispassionately. "No, I don't suppose you were." He returned to the paper. "Legislative assistant to a senator. That's pretty exciting work." He glanced at her sharply. "Why would you settle for a rural community and a shop job after a life like that?"

She swallowed hard. She hadn't expected him to go over the entire page of information about her. She wasn't sure she liked the idea of having her life dissected like this. What was he doing—looking for things to use against her?

No. She stopped herself. She wasn't going to think like that anymore. She would accept him at face value and hope he accepted her the same way.

"It was exciting," she said stiffly. "But I had enough of it. It was also cold and lonely. I enjoy living in a small town where I know everyone and they know and care for me."

He stared at her without comment, then looked back at the application. "I see that you run a shop in town. Would you be willing to give that up in order to work here?"

"I—I'd give everything up," she said a little more passionately than she meant to, then flushed and sank farther back in her chair.

He was staring at her again. If only she could read those brilliant blue eyes!

"Miss Starbuck," he said at last. "I'd like to hire you."

"G-good." Was it? What was he doing? "I think."

"Come along with me," he said rising from behind the desk. "You should take a look at the working environment and see if it suits you."

She followed, a little bewildered. As far as she knew, the wing for the new shops hadn't been built yet. Just where was he taking her?

"Here we are." He'd led her into the living room of the main house. "What do you think of this room?"

She glanced around. Like the other rooms, it was much as it had always been, only fresher and newer looking. "I think it's fine, but—"

"And this?" He led her into the adjacent dining room where she'd eaten a few days before.

"I've always loved this room," she admitted. "But I don't see—"

"Come along." He opened the door to the kitchen and stood back to let her enter. "This one's been remodeled," he explained. "We've put in the most modern appliances available."

She hadn't seen the kitchen on her tour, and this was one aspect of her old house that really had changed. She turned slowly, taking in the double ovens, large microwave and small auxiliary microwave, the double-door refrigerator, the trash compactor. The center of what had once been a fifties-style kitchen had been converted into a long butcher-block counter with separate work centers all around it. A wall had been knocked out and a homey fireplace built to the end of the room. The breakfast nook was still the same, though it needed more plants and the birds were missing.

"I love it," she said.

"Do you think you can work here?" he asked.

What did he think she was applying for, house-keeper?

"Sure," she began. "But, Michael—"

"Come along," he said briskly, ignoring her. "One more room."

She followed him up the stairs and knew before they got there that they were headed for his bedroom. He threw open the door. "Here we are. Do you think you can take care of things in here, too?"

"Michael!" She stared at him, half amused, half appalled.

"Well," he asked, his eyes still cold as Sierra snow, "what do you think? Can you handle the job?"

"Michael, what are you talking about? What does this have to do with running the gift shop?"

He pretended to look surprised. "Running the gift shop?" he said. "But that's not the job description on your application."

"It's not?" Now she was suspicious. "Let me see that."

He handed her the paper and under "position desired" she read "owner's wife" written in heavy red ink. The rest of the application was just as she'd filled it out.

She looked at Michael and didn't know what to do. She wanted to laugh, but his eyes were glacial. Was this a joke or some new sort of torture? She was still on shifting sands, and she didn't know which way to step to safety.

"Th-this is wrong," she began tentatively, but he was on her like a hawk.

"Wrong?" he asked coldly. "You've changed your mind? You don't want the job, after all?"

"Yes. I mean, no." She didn't know what she meant, but she knew this wasn't working out as she'd planned. If she let him go on, who knew where they'd end up? He might tell her that he'd reconsidered, that she didn't quite fit the bill. And then where would she be?

She'd had enough. Instead of trying to untangle things she took the direct approach, fear shimmering through her. She walked slowly toward him and raised her hands to his face, her heart pounding so loud she felt as if the walls should be shaking.

"I don't care about the job," she said, her voice breaking. "Don't you know that? All I want is you." Her love was in her eyes, in the touch of her hands on his cheeks, and if he couldn't read it or didn't want it, she had no more to give.

He stared down at her for a moment that stretched into eternity, and then he placed his own hand over one of hers. "Even if I'm a crook?" he asked gruffly, his gaze suddenly open, exposing a vulnerability that took her breath away.

She nodded, awed by what she saw in him.

"I'm not, you know."

"Yes, I know."

"Good." A smile finally broke through the wintry aspect of his face. "I don't care what the rest of the world thinks as long as you know that."

His arms slid around her, holding her close, and she pressed her face to his chest, love sweeping through her like a sundown wind. "I didn't tell Jeremy about that Oregon town," she said into the warmth of his sweater, wanting him to know everything as quickly as possible. "And I wasn't spying in your room."

"I know that now," he said. "And I don't think I ever seriously believed that you were. But when I saw that pamphlet and then those people from Oregon..."

"Shh," she said, putting a finger to his lips. "It doesn't matter now."

"No, it doesn't." He hugged her more closely, as though afraid to give her enough freedom to get away. "I couldn't possibly think things like that about my wife."

"Oh, Michael!" She felt a giggle coming and couldn't hold it back. After all her fears, this seemed so unreal. "Wife? Do you really want to marry me?"

He looked exasperated. "What else have we been talking about all this time? When I said I wanted you to stay, I meant it." He leaned down and kissed her nose, then each eyelid in turn, as though he couldn't get enough of her. "Besides, if I don't marry you, who's going to redecorate this house? Haven't you noticed that I left everything the way it was? That wasn't because I didn't want to change it. It was because I wanted you to be the one to make the changes."

Michael Donovan's wife. Funny how quickly she was able to get used to that idea. It sounded so right. Just hours earlier her outlook had been so uncertain. What had caused this sudden turnabout? Truth and trust had a lot to do with it. She would have to remember that in the future.

Then she recalled that not all their problems were solved yet. "Oh, but Michael. What about the fire? Who set it?"

He smoothed her hair from her face. "You were right, and I owe you an apology. Jeremy didn't do it."

She sighed with relief, then frowned. "But who did?"

"It was one of the strikers. I'd actually fired him weeks ago, but he came back when he heard about the strike, trying to get revenge. The others turned him in when they realized what he'd done."

Closing her eyes, she pressed her cheek to his sweater. "I'm so glad you weren't hurt," she breathed.

He tipped up her chin with his forefinger. "I'm so glad your house wasn't hurt," he said softly. "If that had happened..."

She smiled at him. "I would have survived," she said, knowing it was true. "But I could never survive losing you."

His kiss sealed their trust and they clung together as though they would never let go again. But even Michael's delicious kisses couldn't last forever, and when he finally released her it was to lead her to the window.

"Look at that," he said, pointing toward the new construction. "In a few days you'll never know there was a fire."

"You're doing quite a job here," she admitted.

He held her close. "And now you'll be doing it with me, helping me decide how to set up the restaurants and shops."

She sighed. "I think I'm going to enjoy that." She frowned as a new thought occurred to her. "I only wish I'd been in on the planning of the stables. You put them in a spot I wish could have been saved."

"That old drainage ditch?" he asked, tousling her hair. "What did you want to save that for?"

"No." She frowned again. "That's not the place I mean."

He grinned. "Well that's where we put them. See for yourself."

She turned to the window and for the first time allowed herself to look toward the hills. There they were—the stables. Right over the old drainage ditch. "But the cemetery..." she gasped.

"Is right where it's always been. Once I got a look at it, I had the plans changed. I wasn't going to risk a haunted horse herd."

She laughed, spinning to hug him. The last of her guilt fell away. Her ancestors couldn't blame her for anything now. "You know what, Michael Donovan?" she asked. "I love you more every minute."

"Good," he answered huskily. "I'm going to give you a chance to prove that."

His kiss was hungry and he pulled her down on the bed, but there was more than lovemaking on his mind. It was the first time since they'd met that they could be together in trust and total freedom. Neither was in a hurry. There was time to learn about each other, time to nourish this fragile, binding emotion they'd discovered together. All the time in the world.

They lay on his bed, holding each other, stroking and talking softly, while the late-afternoon sunlight spilled over them, turning the Blue Room golden to fit their mood.

"Will I get to run the gift shop?" she asked shyly.

"I wouldn't have anyone else do it," he told her. "In fact, I was hoping you'd move your displays out here. You've really created a classy setup."

She nodded happily. "I'm so glad you like them. They'll do much better here at White Acres." She grinned. "And Suzy can keep the ducks."

He laughed, then sobered. "I don't know. Maybe you ought to see if Bernice would like to take over the duck store. Suzy told me she was ready to go to college now. She's had enough of the working life for the time being."

Pamela sighed. "Oh, I'm glad. I was hoping she'd decide to do that." She looked up. "But what about Jeremy?"

"He and I had a long talk and we got some things straightened out between us," he told her. "And then I talked to both of them together. He and Suzy have decided they're not ready to make a lifetime commitment yet. They're going to spend some time apart. He's taking off for Montana."

"Montana?" She rose up on her elbow. "Why Montana?"

Michael shrugged. "He's off to follow some new environmental cause, I suppose. He seems to feel he has to make a success at that somewhere."

"For his father," she murmured, and he nodded. "How about you?" she asked, suddenly brave enough to ask him something truly personal. "Will you prove yourself to your father with White Acres?"

He gazed at her. "Who told you I have anything to prove?" He didn't wait for an answer. "But, yes, I think I will." He ran a hand down the curve of her cheek. "That's not as important to me as some think," he said softly. "There are other things that are much more so."

She closed her eyes and stretched to his touch like a cat before a fire.

"Do you know that I bought this land as much to get you as anything else?" he asked her.

Her eyes flew open. "What do you mean? I didn't come with the land."

He chuckled. "That's just what Mrs. Gimbel said when I told her. I went to see her when I'd decided to buy. I told her I'd met a vision in white on a hill and that had decided me. She laughed and said, 'Pamela Starbuck doesn't come with White Acres,' and I said, 'You want to bet?' I knew even then that I had to have you even more than I had to have the land."

She stared at him. "But you stayed away so long..."

"I knew you'd be upset about losing your home, and I wanted to give you time to get over it before I pressured you. That's why I left you alone as much as I could over the past few months, too. Even though it was hell to stay away." He nibbled on her earlobe. "I took every business trip I could think of—both to get them out of the way, and to have something to keep me from dashing out and carrying you off."

She'd been so blind for so long. How could she make it up to him?

"Just love me," he said as though he'd read her thoughts. "That's all I need."

"I'll love you, Michael Donovan," she whispered, sinking into his embrace. "I'll love you now and forever. You just wait and see."